and other stories

A full list of Terry Pratchett's books
can be found on www.**terrypratchett**.co.uk

TERRY *the fantastically funny* PRATCHETT

DRAGONS
at Crumbling Castle
and other stories

CORGI BOOKS

DRAGONS AT CRUMBLING CASTLE: AND OTHER STORIES
A CORGI BOOK 978 0 552 57280 4

First published in Great Britain by Doubleday,
an imprint of Random House Children's Publishers UK
A Penguin Random House Company

Penguin
Random House
UK

Doubleday edition published 2014
Corgi edition published 2015

1 3 5 7 9 10 8 6 4 2

Text copyright © Terry and Lyn Pratchett, 2014
Illustrations by Mark Beech © RHCP, 2014

All stories contained in this collection were originally published in the 'Children's Circle' section
of the *Bucks Free Press* in the following publication years. All stories were previously untitled, and so
these titles have been attributed for the purposes of this collection.
'Dragons at Crumbling Castle' (1966); 'The Great Speck' (1969); 'Hunt the Snorry' (1966);
'Tales of the Carpet People' (1965); 'Hercules the Tortoise' (1968); 'Dok the Caveman' (1966);
'The Big Race' (1968); 'Another Tale of the Carpet People' (1967); 'The Great Egg-Dancing Championship' (1972);
'Edwo the Boring Knight' (1973); 'The 59A Bus Goes Back in Time' (1966-7); 'The Abominable Snowman' (1969);
'The Blackbury Monster' (1968); 'Father Christmas Goes to Work at the Zoo' (1973)

The right of Terry Pratchett and Mark Beech to be identified as the author and illustrator of
this work has been asserted in accordance with the Copyright, Designs and Patents Act 1988.

Penguin Random House is committed to a sustainable
future for our business, our readers and our planet.
This book is made from Forest Stewardship Council® certified paper.

MIX
Paper from
responsible sources
FSC
www.fsc.org   FSC® C018179

Corgi Books are published by Random House Children's Publishers UK
61–63 Uxbridge Road, London W5 5SA

www.**randomhousechildrens**.co.uk
www.**totallyrandombooks**.co.uk
www.**randomhouse**.co.uk

Addresses for companies within The Random House Group Limited can be found at:
www.**randomhouse**.co.uk/offices.htm

THE RANDOM HOUSE GROUP Limited Reg. No. 954009

A CIP catalogue record for this book is available from the British Library.

Printed and bound by CPI Group (UK) Ltd, Croydon, CR0 4YY

For Colin, who spent far too much of his
time digging around in dusty cupboards to find
all of this material that I had carefully hidden
away and very deliberately forgot all about.
And to my younger self who thought
these stories were pretty good . . .
Oh, I could teach that lad a thing or two!

CONTENTS

INTRODUCTION

Focus on a planet revolving in space . . .

Focus in on a small country in the northern hemisphere – Great Britain.

Closer, closer . . . and on the western edge of London you can see the county of Buckinghamshire. Small villages and winding country roads.

And if you could go back in time to the mid nineteen sixties, you might spot a young lad on a motorbike coming down one such lane, notebook and pen in his jacket pocket.

This is me. A junior reporter for the *Bucks Free Press*, sent out to cover stories on local events. If I was lucky, I would be going to something like a village fair – you know the kind of thing: men putting weasels down their trousers, people bobbing for frogs in a bucket, the odd cheese rolling too fast down a hill . . .

It was a lot of fun back then. And somewhere in the middle of it I taught myself how to write by reading as many books as I could carry home from the library. So then I began writing stories of my own – stories for young readers that were published every week in the newspaper.

The stories in this collection are a selection of those. There are dragons and wizards, councillors and mayors, an adventurous tortoise and a monster in a lake, along with plenty of pointy hats and a few magic spells (a few of which actually do what they are supposed to). Some of these early stories even spawned into my first novel, *The Carpet People*.

So turn the page and read the stories that I wrote as a teenager, mostly as they were first printed, although the grown-up me has tinkered just a *little* with a few fine details – the odd tweak here, a pinch there, and a little note at the bottom where needed, and all because the younger me wasn't as clever back then as he turned out to be.

But that naive young lad on the motorbike and the grown-up me with my black hat and beard are the same person – and all we both ever wanted to do was write for people who are old enough to understand.

And to imagine . . .

Terry Pratchett
Wiltshire, 2014

DRAGONS AT CRUMBLING CASTLE

In the days of King Arthur there were no news-papers, only town criers, who went around shouting the news at the tops of their voices.

King Arthur was sitting up in bed one Sunday, eating an egg, when the Sunday town crier trooped in. Actually, there were several of them: a man to draw the pictures, a jester for the jokes and a small man in tights and football boots who was called the Sports Page.

'DRAGONS INVADE CRUMBLING CASTLE,'

shouted the News Crier (this was the headline), and then he said in a softer voice, **'For full details hear page nine.'**

King Arthur dropped his spoon in amazement. **Dragons!** All the knights were out on quests, except for Sir Lancelot – and he had gone to France for his holidays.

The Ninth Page came panting up, coughed, and said: 'Thousands flee for their lives as family of green dragons burn and rampage around Crumbling Castle . . .'

'What is King Arthur doing about this?' demanded the Editorial Crier pompously. 'What do we pay our taxes for? The people of Camelot demand action . . .'

'Throw them out, and give them fourpence* each,' said the king to the butler. 'Then call out the guard.'

Later that day he went out to the courtyard.

'Now then, men,' he said. 'I want a volunteer . . .' Then he adjusted his spectacles. The only other person in the courtyard was a small boy in a suit of mail much too big for him.

'Ralph reporting, sire!' the lad said, and saluted.

'Where's everyone else?'

'Tom, John, Ron, Fred, Bill and Jack are off

* In the days of King Arthur, this was a lot more money than it seems today – it would buy, oh, at least a cup of mead and a hunk of goat's meat.

sick,' said Ralph, counting on his fingers. 'Then William, Bert, Joe and Albert are on holiday. James is visiting his granny. Rupert has gone hunting. And Eric . . .'

'Well then,' said the king. 'Ralph, how would you like to visit Crumbling Castle? Nice scenery, excellent food, only a few dragons to kill. Take my spare suit of armour – it's a bit roomy, but quite thick . . .'

So Ralph got on his donkey and trotted over the drawbridge, whistling, and disappeared over the hills. When he was out of sight he took off the armour and hid it behind a hedge, because it squeaked and was too hot, and put on his ordinary clothes.

High on a wooded hill sat a mounted figure in coal-black armour. He watched the young boy pass by, then galloped down after him on his big black horse.

'HALT IN THE NAME OF THE FRIDAY KNIGHT,'

he cried in a deep voice, raising his black sword.

Ralph looked round. 'Excuse me, sir,' he said. 'Is this the right road to Crumbling Castle?'

'Well, yes, actually it is,' said the knight, looking rather embarrassed, and then he remembered that he was really a big bad knight, and continued in a hollow voice,

'BUT YOU'LL HAVE TO FIGHT ME FIRST!'

Ralph looked up in amazement as the black knight got off his horse and charged at him, waving his sword.

'Yield!' the knight yelled, then he got his foot stuck in a rabbit hole and tripped over in a great clatter, like an explosion in a tin factory. Bits of armour flew everywhere.

There was silence for a moment, and then the helmet unscrewed itself and Ralph saw that the Friday knight himself was a very small man indeed. Or, at least, he had a very small head.

'Sorry,' said the knight. 'Can I try again?'

'Certainly not!' said Ralph, and unsheathed his rusty sword. 'I've won. You've fallen over first.* It's not even Friday, so I shall call you Fortnight, 'cos I've fought you tonight. You're my prisoner!'

There was a great deal of clanking inside the armour, and then Fortnight climbed out through a trap door in the back. His ferocious black armour was three times as big as he was.

* That's how it went in those days: the first knight to fall over lost the fight. I bet you all knew that.

So Ralph continued his journey to Crumbling Castle on his donkey, followed by Fortnight the Friday knight on his great black charger. After a while they became quite friendly, because Fortnight knew lots of jokes and could sing quite well. He'd belonged to a circus before he became a knight.

Next day they found a wizard sitting on a milestone, reading a book. He had the normal wizard's uniform: long white beard, pointed hat,* a sort of nightdress covered in signs and spells, and long floppy boots, which he had taken off, revealing red socks.

'Excuse me, sir,' said Ralph, because you have to be careful when talking to wizards. 'Is this the way to Crumbling Castle?'

'Thunder and lightning! Yes,' said the wizard, closing his book with a

---

* No self-respecting wizard would be seen in public without a pointy hat. But it could make going through low doorways a bit tricky, so they often developed bad knees in later life due to all that crouching down.

snap. 'Do you mind if I come too? I've got a few anti-dragon spells I'd like to try out.'

He said his name was Fossfiddle, and he was sitting by the road because his magic seven-league boots had broken down. He pointed to the pair of high brown boots by the milestone: magic boots are handy things – you can walk as far as you like in them without getting tired – but Fossfiddle's needed a bit of work on them.

So they gathered round, and since Fossfiddle knew a bit about magic and Fortnight knew a bit about boots and Ralph knew a bit about walking, they soon had the boots working again. Fossfiddle put them on and trotted along by Ralph's donkey.

The land around them grew grimmer and grimmer, and black mountains loomed up on either side. Grey clouds covered the sun, and a cold wind sprang up. The three of them plodded on, and came to a cave hidden in a clump of thorn bushes.

'We could do with a fire,' said Ralph.

'Nothing easier,' said Fossfiddle. He muttered something, and produced a funny-looking glass bulb, a small hat, a banana and a brass candlestick. It wasn't that he was a bad wizard: he just got things mixed up. And if he had but known it, the funny-looking bulb was several centuries ahead of itself.

After Fortnight had lit a fire they settled down around it and Ralph and Fossfiddle dozed off. But Fortnight thought he could hear something.

Crack!

went a stick in the bushes. Something was creeping towards them.

Fortnight picked up his sword and crept towards the bushes. Something was moving in them;

something with very large feet. It was very dark, and somewhere an owl hooted.

'YIELD!'

yelled Fortnight, and dashed into the bushes. This woke up Ralph and Fossfiddle, who heard a great cracking and bashing about going on. So up they got and ran to Fortnight's help.

For five minutes there was no sound to be heard but swishings – and swear words when people trod on thorns. It was so dark nobody knew if anything was creeping up behind them, so they kept turning round and round just to make sure.

'I'VE GOT IT!'

shouted Fortnight, and jumped on something.

'Me!' came Fossfiddle's voice from the leaf-mould.

While all this was going on something very small crawled out of the bushes and began to warm its feet by the fire. Then it rummaged through the rucksacks and ate Fossfiddle's breakfast for tomorrow.

'I heard something, I tell you,' muttered Fortnight, as the three of them came, scratched and bruised, out of the brambles. 'Look, there it is!'

'It's a dragon!' shouted Fossfiddle.

'It's a very weeny one . . .' said Ralph.

The dragon was about the size of a small kettle; it was green and had very large feet. It looked up at them, sniffed a bit, and began to cry.

'Perhaps my breakfast didn't agree with it,' muttered Fossfiddle, looking at his rucksack.

'Well, what shall we do with it?' said Ralph. 'It doesn't look very dangerous, I must say.'

'Has it lost its mummy then?' cooed Fortnight, getting down on his hands and knees and smiling at it. It backed away, and breathed some smoke at

him. Fortnight wasn't very good with children.

Finally they made it a bed in a big saucepan, put the lid on, and went back to sleep.

When they set off next morning Fossfiddle carried the saucepan on his back. After all, they couldn't just leave the dragon behind. After a while the lid opened, and the dragon stared out.

'This isn't dragon country,' said Ralph. 'I suppose it must have got lost.'

'It's the green variety. They grow to be thirty feet tall,' said Fortnight, 'and then they take to roaring and rampaging and walking on the grass and other lawlessness and wicked deeds.'

'What sort of deeds?' asked Ralph interestedly.

'Oh – well, I don't know. Leaving taps running and slamming doors, I suppose.'

That afternoon they came to Crumbling Castle.

It was on a high hill all by itself, and built of grey stone. In the valley below was a town, but most of it was burned down. There was no sign of anybody, not even a dragon.

They plucked up the courage to knock at the big black door. Fortnight's knees were knocking, and since he was wearing armour, this made a terrible din.

'There's no one in,' he said quickly. 'Let's go back!'

The door wouldn't open, so Fossfiddle got out his spell book.

'Hopscotchalorum, Trempledingotram- lines!' he chanted. 'Open!'

Instead the door turned into pink meringue. Fossfiddle always got things wrong.

'My word, dashed tasty door that,' said Fortnight, when they finally got through. They were in an empty courtyard. It seemed they were being watched. 'I don't like this much,' he added, looking around and drawing his sword. 'I get the feeling that something is going to jump out on us.'

'That's very nice, I must say,' said Fossfiddle, whose nerves were not as good as they had been.

'It's all right,' said Ralph. 'Dragons are seldom bigger than the average house and not much hotter than the average furnace.' He trod on Fossfiddle's cloak as the wizard tried to run away. 'So come back.'

Just then they met a dragon. It looked quite like the one asleep in the saucepan in Fossfiddle's pack, except it was much **MUCH** bigger.

It crawled across the courtyard to them.

'**Morning,**' it said.

Now this placed our heroes in a bit of a quandary, as you can see. You can't go off and kill something that's just said good morning to you.

'Good morning,' said Ralph, rather embarrassed. 'I suppose we've come to the right place?'

'**Yes, this is Crumbling Castle. I suppose you've come about all these people who've been bothering us.**'

'First we've heard,' said Ralph. 'We heard that you dragons were bothering people. Where is everyone, anyway?'

The old dragon yawned. '**Down at the dragon caves.**'

Then he explained it all to them. Dragons were really quite peaceful, and these had been living in some caves down by the river, bothering no one except the fish, which they ate. But then the lord of the castle had built a dam downriver, and their caves had been flooded out.

So the dragons had come to live in the castle, scaring everyone else away. They had burned a few houses down, but they always checked that there was no one at home before they did so.

While the old dragon was talking, other dragons came from various parts of the castle and sat around listening.

'And now they've come and kidnapped the dragon prince,' said the dragon.

'Is he about twelve inches long, with large paws and a habit of biting?' said Fossfiddle suspiciously. 'Because if he is, we found him a few days ago. He'd just got lost.' He held out the saucepan, and the little dragon hopped out.

There had to be a lot of explaining. Fortnight went down to the river and found the lord hiding up a tree, and brought him back. Most of the other castle people followed the lord.

'I'm afraid there's no possibility of taking the dam down,' said the lord, hiding behind Fortnight. 'We built it for a swimming pool.'

'You don't have to,' said Ralph. 'All you need to do is build a few caves out of bricks or something.'

So they did. The three fighters pitched in and helped, and it wasn't long before they had a nice row of caves, with hot and cold running water and a bath in each one. The dragons took to them at once, and agreed to leave the castle.

'I suppose that's it then,' said Ralph, as they strolled away from the castle with all the dragons and people waving to them.

'Good job for the dragons there wasn't any fighting,' said Fossfiddle, 'or they might have found out a thing or two!'

They had a good laugh about that, and disappeared over the hill.

THE GREAT SPECK

Have you ever looked around the room on a sunny day and seen little specks of dust floating in the air? They look like stars when the light catches them, and the very small people that live on them think that's what the others are.

The one particular speck I'm thinking of was about one hundredth of a millimetre long, and was called Great Speck. There were two countries on it – Grabist, on the left-hand side, and Posra, on the right. In the middle was a range of very small mountains.

On the highest lived an astronomer called Gwimper, who, as Great Speck floated around, watched all the other specks with great interest. Of course, no one believed that life existed on the other dust motes. Then one day Gwimper thought he saw something, on a speck not far away.

'What's that?' asked the King of Posra, while Gwimper stood before him waving his arms and pointing.

'Trees!,

gasped the astronomer.

'Mountains!

Animals!'

'Hmm,' said the king. 'About how far away is it?'

Gwimper went through his pockets until he found a piece of paper, covered with sums. 'It's heading towards Great Speck at one-sixty-fourth of a millimetre per second, and it will pass within two centimetres of us in thirty seconds,' he said.

A second was about as long as a day for the Speck people.

At the same moment Winceparslie, another astronomer, was saying exactly the same thing to the Duke of Grabist.

Now, Great Speck has been at peace for – oh, at least half an hour, but that is not to say that either country would be above pulling a fast one on the other if it got the chance.

So both countries immediately set about finding

ways of getting to the new speck without letting the other know.

'But how?' asked Gwimper. Since they were so small the people naturally floated, but the problem was to propel themselves across the two centimetres. He finally built a sort of covered-in rowing boat with two pairs of wings and a lot of ornamental carving.

'What a splendid-looking craft!' said the king, when it was brought to him. 'I can see you will enjoy the trip.'

There was a thoughtful silence.

'Me?' asked Gwimper.

'But yes!' said the king.

'I thought we ought to kind of send some animals or something to find out if it's safe,' began Gwimper nervously.

'I'm sure you'll find out,' said the king heartily,

slapping him on the back.

Gwimper walked miserably back to his observatory and peered up at the new speck. It was already bigger. What would happen if he missed, and got lost? He shuddered when he looked into the infinite immensity of the air, and saw the millions of dust motes up there.

Meanwhile, the king's servants dragged the flying machine up to a small hill overlooking the palace, and filled it full of provisions.

Then they put a fence round it and charged people who wanted to come and look.

The second of the Great Leap grew nearer . . .

'Where's Gwimper?' cried the King of Posra as the second arrived. 'I've got to pin a medal on him before he takes off (I don't expect there'll be a chance to do it when he comes back).'

The crowds were all gathered around the astronomer's flying machine, which was called the *Anybody*.

But Gwimper was nowhere to be seen.*

Then at last he appeared, looking very sheepish in an outsize flying helmet and goggles. The band immediately struck up the Posrian national anthem,

'Three Cheers for Us',

and the king threw a huge tin medal round his neck like a hoopla hoop, where it hung sadly on a red ribbon.

* But he could be heard. For the toilets nearby had been occupied for a Very Long Time, and a lot of flushing noises were coming out of there.

'Well, goodbye, old friend,' said the king. 'Remember to plant the Posrian flag on that new speck. We've put a gramophone record of the national anthem in the *Anybody*. I understand that Grabist is sending a flying machine too. I don't need to tell you that you'll land first, *HINT*, *HINT*, do I?'

Gwimper climbed into the *Anybody* and started the engine.

A runway had been built down the side of one hill and halfway up another one. The idea was that the *Anybody* would gather speed and whizz up the hill and away from Great Speck.

Or it might crash.

Suddenly the crowd rushed up and gave it a jolly good push. They didn't care – anything for a laugh was their motto.

Gwimper hung on tightly when the *Anybody* shot up the hill, felt his stomach turn over, and next moment the flying machine was flapping quietly through the air.

I don't quite believe it, he thought, looking out of the rear window. Great Speck was floating quite a way away. And someone was behind him, banging on the hatch. It turned out to be the king.

'THEY DIDN'T WAIT TO PUSH TILL I GOT OFF!'

he shrieked as Gwimper let him scramble in.

'TAKE ME BACK!'

'I'm not sure if I can,' said Gwimper, who was secretly pleased. 'Great Speck is rushing away from us. If you remember, I did tell you that I probably wouldn't be able to get back.'

'Did you? What did we say?'

'You told me not to worry, your majesty.'

The king looked out of the window. There was nothing but Nothing all around them. A few distant dust specks glittered, and far, far below was the hill they had taken off from.

'Can't we signal them?' said the king.

'Actually, I did work out a way to signal back to Great Speck,' said Gwimper. He opened a cupboard and produced two flags, then opened the window and started semaphoring to the fast-disappearing speck of dust.

'My assistant is tracking us through the telescope,' he said, waving his arms. 'I've just signalled: "The King (May He Live For Ever, etc., etc., etc.,) is alive and well and up here with me." Now just pass me that little telescope, sire. That's right. Let's see now . . . Ah, yes. The reply is: "Get him down again, you crazy booby." But I'm afraid I can't.'

'How far have we gone?' asked the king.

Gwimper twiddled some dials. 'About seven-eighteenths of a centimetre,' he said. 'Not bad going.'

The king took off his crown. 'I was a bit of an adventurer in my youth,' he said wistfully. 'Can I be the first one to set foot on this new speck?'

'Certainly,' said Gwimper generously.

'Right, then. Tell me how the controls work.'

Soon the king was flying the *Anybody* and enjoying himself tremendously.

When the new speck appeared, Gwimper put the *Anybody* into orbit.

'I think we'll call it New Speck,' said the king, as they looked down at it. 'Look, there are some mountains and things. I wonder if anything lives down there?'

The *Anybody* floated slowly down, and landed with a slight bump.

'ME FIRST!'

shouted the king, and jumped out with the Posrian flag in his hand.

Gwimper followed slowly, carrying a gramophone, and the two of them stood to attention while it played a rather scratchy record of the Posrian national anthem, **'Three Cheers for Us'**.

'Right,' said the king. 'You take a photo of me and I'll take one of you.'

But Gwimper was busily breaking up bits of dust with a hammer, and looking at them through a microscope, so the king wandered off by himself.

New Speck was quite rough, with boulders and large stones everywhere. Soon the king sat down on one and watched the astronomer collecting plants in a canvas bag. The rock stood up, shook him off, and ran away on four stumpy little legs.

'Remarkable!' said Gwimper.

'**OUCH!**' cried the king.

'Look, there's another of them.' A rock had opened two little beady eyes, and sat looking at them.

Then they heard, a long way off, a recorder being played rather badly. Gwimper and the king stared at each other, and as the music went on they began to realize what it was:

'*. . . perish her enemies,*
By Fire, the Sword, Drowning, etc.,
Grabist the Brave! (Pom-te-pom!)'

'It's the clugging Grabistian national anthem,' raged the king. 'The wootling mousesherters have been and gone and got here!'

'Ssssh!' hissed Gwimper, peering over the rocks.

There he saw, in a little valley, a flying machine very like the *Anybody*, with the name *Everybody* written on it. He recognized the Grabistian astronomer, Winceparslie, and standing next to him, winding up the gramophone again, was the Duke of Grabist.

'The great ninnygremblers!' cursed the king. 'Landing on our speck of dust! Let's put them to the sword! Perish their enemies, indeed!'

He was shouting so loudly that soon the duke and the astronomer came bounding over the hill.

'**You!**' said everyone at once.

'Get off our New Speck!' bellowed the duke and the king together. 'This means war!' they added.

'**Beastly trespasser!**'
'**Claim-jumper!**'

Winceparslie and Gwimper wandered off, leaving the other two shouting and jumping up and down.

'I'm worried about how we're getting back,' confided Winceparslie.

'Me too.'

'This doesn't look like a very pleasant place,' Winceparslie said, waving his hand at the rocks and the little stone creatures.

'Very bleak, yes.'

'I can't help thinking their majesties are getting worked up about nothing.'

'What are we going to do about it?'

At that moment there was a rumbling noise, and a herd of the stone creatures came charging up the valley and trampled over the Grabistian machine.

'Oh no! The *Everybody* is destroyed!' Winceparslie whimpered.

The creatures surged over the hill. There was another crash.

'There goes the *Anybody* too,' moaned Gwimper. 'Now we're both stuck.'

They rushed over the hill to find the king and the duke building a wall, and shouting at each other over the top of it.

'Our ships have been destroyed!' shouted Gwimper.

'Come over onto our side of the wall and stop consorting with the enemy,' said the king.

'WE CAN'T GET BACK HOME!'

screamed Winceparslie at the top of his voice.

There was a sudden silence. The king and the duke looked up at the distant specks of dust.

'The Great Speck is three centimetres away and getting further with every micro-second,' said Gwimper. 'Even if they built another ship they could never rescue us and get back. We're stuck. Those stone things have trodden on the ships, and there are no spare parts. Right. Now what are we going to *do*?'

'Are you sure the ships are wrecked?' asked the duke.

'They're ruined,' said Winceparslie.

'Then we're stuck – and I don't like this place,' said the king.

Gwimper looked at the remains of the *Anybody* and the *Everybody* and had an idea. 'I wonder if we could take them both apart and make another one with the pieces,' he said.

So while the king and the duke sat by a small fire, the two astronomers started taking the flying machines apart. They used the hull, gas stove, steering wheel and seats from the *Anybody*, and the wings, motor and instruments from the *Everybody*.

While they were working the king caught one of the stone creatures, but there didn't seem to be any way of eating it. All that was left of the provisions in the ships was half a loaf of bread, some rather smelly cheese, and – no one knew why – a box of glacé cherries.*

'Stop fighting over them, anyway,' said Gwimper. 'We think we've got a working ship.'

They all climbed into the ship, which Winceparslie had named *Somebody*, and Gwimper pulled a few levers. The wings flapped and the ship rose.

'Well, goodbye, New Speck,' said the king. 'I'm glad to leave, even though it belongs to me.'

---

* It's a rule of the known universe that every kitchen in the world anywhere has a box of glacé cherries hiding somewhere in it. No one knows why.

'To me, you mean!' said the duke, waving his arms.

The ship hovered over the speck of dust while the astronomers looked around for Great Speck.

'That's it!' said Gwimper. 'The green one, floating over there by the Table.'

The *Somebody* speeded up, and it wasn't long before it landed in the mountains that separated the country of Posra from Grabist. The king and the duke rushed out and away down the mountains in opposite directions.

'Here we go again,' said Winceparslie, as he helped unload the ship. 'They'll be arguing again tomorrow. Argue, argue, argue. You'd think they might have learned their lesson by now. They might have learned to *co-operate*.'

'They might still,' said Gwimper thoughtfully. 'I've just noticed something. They were so eager to

get home they each ran down the wrong side of the mountains. The duke has gone into Posra and the king has run down into Grabist!'

'Gosh! What'll happen to them?'

'Oh, they might get put in prison for a little while, but I dare say the people will swap them. Though one duke's as good as another, if you ask me.'

And they went and had a cup of tea in Gwimper's observatory, and played chess together until midnight.

HUNT THE SNORRY

The Great Expedition to find the Snorry began to assemble at the harbour one misty morning.

Colonel Vest, the famous little-game* hunter, told the men from the newspapers (who all had to get up at three in the morning to see him off): 'No one is quite sure what the Snorry looks like, so we'll be able to tell them when we find it. Some people say that it's covered in blue fur; others say it tends

* Basically, anything smaller than himself, and preferably no taller than his knee.

to sneeze a lot. One man who thought he had seen it said it made a loud whistling noise and ran around in circles. Personally, I think it lives in trees and waggles its ears. Anyway, that's what we're going to find out.'

The expedition certainly looked as if it was going to find out something. The dock was piled high with nets, various traps, ropes, self-inflatable canoes, pieces of old string and giant crates of tapioca, said by some to be the Snorry's favourite food.

Besides Colonel Vest there was a camera-man, a doctor, a botanist, a plumber, a scissor manu-facturer, a knife-grinder, a man called Harris, who was very good at French verbs, and eighty-three other people. Whatever the Snorry turned out to be, there was bound to be someone in the party who could watch it, catch it, talk to it, or throw things at it. They set sail . . .

*

The Snorry's haunt was said to be in the giant tapioca forests of the Upper Amazon, and Colonel Vest led his party there.

For days and days they trudged on, through rather murky swamps full of mosquitoes, and trackless jungles where they spent most of their time following one another round in circles. People they met said yes, this was just the sort of place you caught a Snorry in, and then they went away and laughed quietly to themselves.

After a few weeks they had come right up to the place where the Amazon was no more than a little trickle, and the giant tapioca trees loomed all around them. Still there was no sign of a Snorry, and at least three people had disappeared. Probably the Snorry had got them.

Harris had suffered a particularly nasty shock too when he trod on an alligator. Even worse, the alligator could not understand a single French verb when he tried to talk to it.

'I give up,' said Colonel Vest, sitting down on a log and sneezing. 'Does anybody have any idea yet what the Snorry looks like?'

No one had, and they all sat down and waited for something to happen. After weeks of traipsing through wet tapioca forests they all felt pretty miserable, and most of them were sneezing a lot.

A small man who came wandering through the forest collecting fallen tapioca in a sack stopped to look at them.

'I see you've all caught a Snorry,' he said.

'Have we?' They all looked rather puzzled. 'What is it then?'

'Well,' he replied with a smile. '*We* call it a Snorry – but I suppose *you* would call it a bad cold.'

TALES OF THE CARPET PEOPLE

To the Carpet people the Carpet was bigger than a forest, and was full of cities, towns, small villages, castles and all sorts of tiny animals – even cunning and hairy bandits in the really thick parts that weren't swept often. Snibril, however, lived on the edge of the Carpet, and the Carpet was fraying. That was something everyone knew. In the village of the Fallen Matchstick, the Carpet-dwellers were already preparing to leave. The only question was – where could they go?

Snibril galloped back along the line of wagons that stood waiting in the main street of the village, loaded with chairs, stoves, beds, and anything else that people could tie onto them, which included almost everything.

Snibril tied his bounder – a rather nervous animal that looked like a grasshopper – up at the post outside the council hall and went inside. The whole village was there waiting for him, but mostly waiting to meet the white-haired old Carpet-dweller who Snibril had brought with him, clinging desperately to the back of the bounder.

'Gentlemen,' said Snibril, 'this is Pismire the hermit, who used to live in a cave at Underlay. He thinks he knows a way to help us.'

'Don't rush me, please,' said Pismire. 'My grandfather's grandfather was Robinson the Wanderer, of whom you have all heard . . . ?' There was a question at the end of that statement, the kind of question that meant you jolly well *ought* to have heard of his grandfather's grandfather.

'Wasn't he the one who was supposed to have walked across the Carpet?' said Snibril.

'Yes, right across and back again. Well, before he died, he told my grandfather about his journey. He said there was a land where no one lived, but which would be a perfect place for Carpet-dwellers.'

'And where is that?' asked Glurk the hunter.

Pismire pointed. 'Over there, gentlemen. Right on the other side of the Carpet.'

'The other side of the Carpet! That would mean going right round the edge, wouldn't it?' said Glurk.

'No, our supplies wouldn't last that long,' Snibril said. 'We must go across the middle, like Pismire's great-great-grandfather did. What he did, we can do. I know the Carpet is unexplored and full of dangers, and strange lands, and all the rest, but I don't think we have any choice. The Carpet can and must be crossed.'

An hour later Snibril rode his bounder up to the first cart in the line. Looking back, he could see the people climbing onto their wagons, and looking sadly around at the village they were leaving. Many of them were wondering what would lie ahead in the unknown parts of the Carpet.

'Follow me!' he cried, waving his hat in the air.

'Across the Carpet!'

'Across the Carpet,' they answered, as the carts slowly creaked forward. 'Across the Carpet!'

*

Snibril and Glurk rode their bounders along a fallen Carpet hair, watching the laden carts trundle by far beneath them. Although they had not been journeying long, the Carpet hairs were already thicker and grew closer together, and there were dark shadows between them.

'It's very quiet,' said Snibril thoughtfully.

'I wish it was noisy,' growled Glurk. 'When it's this quiet it gives me forebodings. Listen.'

'You mean the creaking of the carts?' said Snibril, after a while.

'Not that. There is something else.'

Snibril listened. Then, above the creaking, he could hear something. Far away, and very faint, like a far-off drumming.

'Carpet-messages,' said Glurk. 'The news of us will be passed from drum to drum right across the Carpet. There'll be trouble, you mark my words. Whatever is drumming doesn't like us on its territory.'

'It will take more than drumming to stop us.'

'There will be more than drumming. I feel it in my bones.'

Snibril urged his bounder down the hair to the line of moving carts, and galloped up to the front wagon, where Pismire was steering. He looked at Pismire, then turned in the saddle. 'We're stopping here! Get the carts round in a circle!'

Soon the animals were unharnessed and the carts had creaked into place. Here and there, on top of carts and in the shadows, sat armed bowmen, with the long thin bows that had made the hunters of the Fallen Matchstick famous. Fires sprang up all around the circle, and soon there were smells of stews and soups – and the roasting of fresh meat caught that day when Glurk had taken some bowmen out hunting in the hair-thickets. Snibril and Pismire ate with the Glurk family.

'Good soup, this,' said Glurk, drinking noisily. 'I wonder what the hunting will be like across the Carpet. Now, what I always say . . . **What in Weft's name was that?'**

There was silence for a moment, broken only by the youngest child coughing on some soup that had gone down the wrong way. All around the circle people had stopped talking, and were reaching for their bows.

Then they heard it again: a long, thin **howl** that echoed from hair to hair in the dark Carpet.

In the shadows beyond the bright circle many pairs of tiny, evil red eyes were watching . . .

Glurk snatched up his bow and peered into the darkness beyond the circle. 'Snargs!'

'What's a snarg?' asked Snibril, fitting a bolt into his crossbow.

'Hunt in packs,' puffed Glurk, his bow twanging. 'Mainly claws and teeth. Can't stand the light and hate anyone who can – hurry up with those arrows there!'

Snibril watched as the people formed themselves into the traditional Carpet-fighting formation. A squad of bowmen stood by the fires, lighting the ends of their arrows. Then there was a *twang* and a loud **whoosh!** and half a dozen fire-arrows rose above the clearing, lighting up the darkness. Then every bowman could fire at the first snarg he saw. It usually worked quite well.*

Glurk was sitting on a wagon and cursing each time he missed, and his newest wife was handing him up arrow after arrow. Snibril and Gurth (Glurk's

* When it didn't, no one came back to say so, anyway.

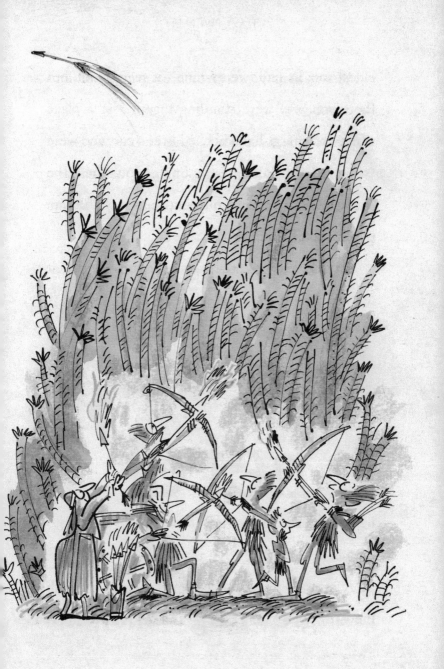

eldest son; he had twenty-nine – it seems a lot, but there you are) were standing together at a place where the snargs had knocked over a cart and were trying to get into the circle. Snibril could hear the sound of snarg bodies pushing their way through the Carpet, hemming the tribe in.

Another flight of fire-arrows went up. Snibril felt for an arrow, then realized he had used them all.

'Help, here!'

he yelled, as he and Gurth took a flying leap onto the nearest cart.

A mass of black bodies were pushing through the gap, **growling** and snarling.

Then they stopped, their evil red eyes watching the people. Arrows clattered harmlessly off their thick skins.

Then the biggest snarg, the leader of the pack, leaped forward until it was alone in the middle of the clearing.

'It's looking for someone to fight,' whispered Glurk to Pismire. 'And it might as well be me.'

'I don't think that will be necessary,' said Pismire, pointing.

Someone had stepped into the firelight, holding a large carving knife. It was Snibril.

The snarg chief seemed to laugh, then the two started to circle each other.

The snargs and the people watched as the chief snarg prepared to spring. But as it did so, Snibril ducked, and as the giant body whizzed over him, he threw the knife upwards as hard as he

could. The snarg landed, skidded along on its face for a little way, then rolled over with its legs in the air. Dead.

A howl went up from the snarg pack, and they began to creep forward, glaring at Snibril.

'Enough!' shouted someone, and something swung across the circle on a Carpet-creeper to pick Snibril up by his hair and drop him on a cart. Then it swung back, and leaped down in front of the snargs. Whoever it was put a long shining stick to his shoulder, and took aim.

The snargs crept forward, as the strange figure raised the metal tube.

With a large bang and a cloud of smoke the figure fell over backwards – and so, happily, did five or six snargs. The rest bolted, howling.

The newcomer picked himself up, blew down

his tube, coughed, and walked over to them.

'My name is Bane—' he began, but Glurk interrupted him.

'Yes, you are a Wanderer. Only Wanderers carry the ancient guns of the Shiandian Empire. I am proud to meet you.'

'Thank you. And you are Glurk, renowned across the Carpet as a brave and courageous hunter. You are Snibril, a Carpet-dweller with more imagination than most. And you are Pismire, wisest among Carpet-dwellers.' He looked at them all and grinned. 'I have been following you for inches.'

'We saw nobody,' said Snibril.

'People don't, not if I'm following them, and you talk loudly and don't shield your fires. Be thankful that you have met nothing more terrible than a few snargs.'

Pismire went white. 'Do you mean there are worse things?'

'Look, this is no time for talking. Get some sleep and we'll leave by first light. Take some of those snargs too; they make a passable stew, if simmered.'

Early the next morning the people were moving on again, putting as much distance as possible between themselves and the clearing. Snibril's bounder trotted along at the head of the procession, and Bane walked beside it. He was wearing a battered snarg-skin hat, a small bundle on his back, and carried his gun over his shoulder.

'In the old days,' he was saying, 'when the city of Shiandi ruled half the Carpet from the Land beneath the Bookcase, the original Wanderers were explorers, guides, and kept some sort of order on the Carpet-fringes. At that time this track we can hardly get along was a broad road, crowded with traders and soldiers. But alas, after the great battle between Shiandi and the people of the South-West Chairleg, the Empire collapsed.

'Now there are very few Wanderers, and most don't bother to hand their old guns on to their sons; those of us left are looked upon as tramps, which we are really.'

'What happened to Shiandi?'

'It still exists. So does the city at the South-West Chairleg, and both armies have been seen again. That's why I've been following you. Because my spies tell me that both armies have heard of some people who are looking for a new kind of land across the Carpet. Both Shiandi Beneath the Bookcase and the City of the South-West Chairleg want that land, for whoever gets it will be powerful enough to finally beat the other. In other words, they are looking for the people of the Fallen Matchstick. Or, to put it another way, you.'

Camp had been struck, and except for a few guards who stood with their knees knocking, the people attended the special council of war outside Glurk's wagon. Something had to be done. Glurk was making a speech, with much pulling of his moustache and waving of hands in the air.

'So the point is this,' he finished. 'If we are found by these armies that Bane says are looking for us, we won't stand a chance. After all, we are pioneers, not soldiers.'

The crowd around the table was silent, and then a Carpet-dweller named Blint stepped forward, and coughed nervously.

'Perhaps we had better turn back?' he whispered.

'No!' Snibril leaped to his feet and banged

on the table. 'No turning back now! We left our homes to come this far – we can't go back. Haven't we a dream of this land? Then we must be prepared to fight for it, against all the armies in the Carpet if necessary. Who agrees with me?'

Glurk and Pismire immediately went to stand behind Snibril; slowly, family by family, all the others followed them, including an embarrassed Blint. Bane, who did not count himself as one of them, sat polishing his gun and whistling between his teeth. No one ever found *him* cursing and flapping his ears in amazement.

'Right,' said Snibril. 'Now I have a plan. These armies are waiting somewhere to attack us. If they do, we will lose. But they don't expect us to do one thing.'

'What?' asked Pismire.

'Attack them first! Keep the wagons moving,

but a few spies go out ahead. I'll be one of them. Then, if we spot anything, we can come back and warn the people, and then try and stop the army finding us. Pismire, you'll be needed here. You too, Glurk, and don't argue. Bane . . .'

'I was waiting for that,' said Bane, slinging his gun over his shoulder. 'We'd best go now.'

Snibril got his crossbow and a full quiver of arrows, stuck two swords and a club in his belt, a spear in either hand, and a knife between his teeth. Bane smiled, and removed them all except the bow and the sword.

'A Wanderer never clutters himself up,' he said. 'We outnumber them two to two thousand as it is.'*

A short while later the two of them had climbed a hair, cut themselves Carpet-creepers – Bane taught Snibril this useful trick – and swung softly off into the darkness.

* Most people would have preferred it the other way round.

*

After dark the Carpet was a dangerous place to be in. Little beady eyes looked out of every shadow, and strange things clomped and snuffled in the darkness. Here and there round the edge of the Carpet winked tiny pinpoints of light, where an isolated village slept behind strong barricades. Every time a distant snarg **howled** people shook in their beds, and pitied anyone out in the Carpet on such a night.

Snibril and Bane slept halfway up a hair, one watching while the other rested. Something large and black seemed to be dancing around the bottom of the hair, blowing its nose menacingly. Snibril didn't know what it was, but he was glad when it went away.

Peering down, Snibril thought he could see a light in the hairs, and hear drums beating. Suddenly the light rounded a hair and came into full view, and he could see hundreds of torches marching together, shining off armour and spears.

He woke Bane, who spent a long time looking through his portable telescope.

'That's the Shiandian army all right,' said Bane. 'Or some of it at any rate.'

'It's quite big enough for me! What are we going to do about it?'

'They seem to be camping here for the night, so we'd best wait till morning. However . . .' Bane looked thoughtfully down at the army, which was making camp, setting up tents, and lighting fires. Interesting smells rose from the camp-kitchens, and Snibril thought sadly of the meagre rations he carried in his pack. 'I wonder why there aren't that many of them,' Bane continued. 'I don't trust them. I wonder if the wagons are in any danger?'

'Well, they are about an inch south of here. They should be safe— **Great galloping snargs!** Look!'

Through the dark there came another army, or rather the other half of the first one. And between each platoon of soldiers was a wagon – Snibril recognized them. On the first wagon, looking very

miserable, sat Pismire and Glurk, who could hardly be seen for ropes.

'How did they do it?' moaned Snibril.

'Ambushed them, I shouldn't wonder,' muttered Bane between clenched teeth. 'Wait till I get my hands on 'em! I'll teach 'em to harm innocent travellers while I'm around!'

'What will they do now?'

'Take them back to Shiandi for questioning, I shouldn't wonder. And when they do, we're going with them!'

A few hours later, when the complete army and their prisoners started back to the city, search parties were sent out to make sure they weren't followed. But they didn't notice two grey shapes swinging from hair to hair, high above their heads . . .

The city of Shiandi had been carved, long ago, out of a speck of dust. It had many tall, black towers, and was surrounded by a high black wall with only one gate. The Carpet around the city was dark and shadowy.

In through the great gate of Shiandi marched

the Shiandian army, dressed in black and gold armour, their marching echoing between the dark walls. The carts of the people were dragged in too, and the black gate closed with a final clang!

Two pairs of eyes peered out of the hairs near the gate.

'There aren't any guards,' whispered Snibril.

'They never bother to guard Shiandi. They put all their trust in the walls. If you'll just follow me, however . . .' Bane tiptoed into a nearby thicket and Snibril heard him cutting a small piece of hair. Then Bane came running out with the hair held in front of him, stuck it in the Carpet in front of the wall, sprang into the air and disappeared over the top.

A few seconds later Snibril had followed him,* and then they swung themselves hand over hand along a ledge until they reached a window.

They were looking into the Great Hall, and the

---

* Luckily it was a soft landing and not pointy sticks on the other side.

first thing Snibril saw was Glurk, bound and held by five soldiers. On the steps leading up to the emperor's throne stood a bound Pismire, looking defiantly at the emperor, a thin Carpet-dweller in a crown and long robes.

'For the last time, where is this land?' screamed the emperor.

Pismire said nothing.

'Tell me!'

'Shan't.'

'Guards! I've had enough of this one. Take him down to the cells with the others. We'll soon get the truth out of him—'

'Stop that!' yelled Snibril.

They all turned to look up in surprise.

Before anyone realized what was happening the soldier within kicking distance of Pismire had his toes trodden on. While the soldier was hopping about Pismire removed his sword, and with one mighty hack cut his ropes to free himself. While Glurk was making short work of the guards near him, the other two climbed down into the hall, and the fight was on.

The four of them stood together like . . . well, whenever they tell stories around the campfire, Carpet-dwellers always speak of that battle with hushed voices.

It was soon over, but more guards were battering on the doors.

'Which way to the cells?' panted Bane, dragging Pismire away from the emperor, who was sitting on the back of his throne and screaming.

'Down,' said Glurk, pointing to a dark tunnel. The four of them rushed down it just as the doors of the hall burst open. A gaoler, who looked up to see four ferocious fighters bearing down on him, dropped his keys and ran. Glurk and Pismire ran from cell to cell, unlocking the heavy doors and releasing the more revengeful people.

'The carts are still in the courtyard,' cried Snibril. **'Follow me!'**

It did not take long for the people to fight their way up to the courtyard where the carts were. They were used to fighting in narrow spaces, and Carpet people have sharp teeth and claws, when they want to use them.

Snibril, Glurk and Bane (and Pismire, who had just decided to become a soldier) ran up the steps leading to the gatehouse tower. A few soldiers were there, but not for long.

Snibril grabbed one as he ran past. 'Open the gate,' he said.

'This is no time for half measures,' said Bane, prodding the prisoner in the ear with his gun. 'Tell us how to open the gate, if you please, or I will blow your head off.'

He said it quite quietly, but the soldier gulped, and slowly turned the windlass that opened the gate.

As the gate rose the first cart went trundling out, and cart after cart followed, going as fast as any cart had a right to. Any soldiers who were foolish enough to keep on fighting were cuffed and thrown into the bushes. When the last cart bounced out of Shiandi the four fighters swung down over the wall and landed on it.

*

The chase was something that Snibril remembered all his life. The carts were not built for speed, but they tore through the Carpet so fast that he expected the wheels to fly off in all directions. And, a long way behind, he could hear the army.

'What now?' he shouted, as they clung onto the jolting roof.

'What indeed,' said Bane. 'I think we are heading towards the Swinging Bridge. There is a great gap in the Carpet, and the bridge is a single hair that crosses it. I think that it is just wide enough for a cart to cross.'

'Oh dear,' said Pismire.

It *was* just wide enough, but Pismire happened to look over the edge of the cart as it crossed the bridge, and found himself staring right down through the Carpet. After that he didn't look down again.

Snibril looked back once they were over, and saw the soldiers coming up to the bridge. They were going to cross!

'Over my dead body,' he muttered, and jumped off the cart. He ran out to the middle of the bridge and drew his sword. Bane saw him go and, without being seen, jumped off the cart and slipped into the bushes.

Snibril stood alone in the middle of the thin, high bridge, and swished his sword about a bit to make it quite clear what would happen to the first soldier that crossed.

For a peaceful Carpet-dweller Snibril looked furious as he advanced along the narrow bridge. The leading soldiers had to move back, which pushed them up against the soldiers at the back who were trying to get to the front to see what was going on.

Meanwhile Bane had spat on his hands and

gripped the end of the bridge. His eyes crossed and his muscles twanged like bowstrings as he took the weight, until he was holding the end above his head. His feet began to sink into the Carpet.

'Come back, Snibril,'

he cried. 'I'm going to topple the bridge!'

Snibril gave one last swish with his sword, so that the leading soldier backed into someone else's spear again, and ran for the end of the bridge.

As he jumped down Bane took a deep breath and hurled the end of the bridge away from him.

It hung there, poised for a moment, then **crashed** and rumbled down into the gap until it could no longer be seen. Soldiers tumbled with it, some clinging desperately to handholds in the fallen hair and trying to scramble back up to safety.

'From now on,' said Bane, as they sat on the

leading cart, 'we must not stop. We are leaving Shiandi territory now, and I don't think they'll dare follow us into the unknown regions – but have a care! It wouldn't take them long to get round the tear and follow us. And when the bounders get tired, put them on the carts and carry the carts.

We must not stop!'

'What about the other enemy?' said Glurk. 'We seem to have avoided them so far. Are we safe?'

'You never know in the Carpet. You're never really safe anyway. But be prepared to fight a bit more. Worthwhile things aren't just there for the taking, you know.'

They sat in silence for a while, listening to the creaking of the carts and the far-off drums that were always the background noises in the dark regions of the Carpet. There were other things – distant roaring, bright eyes that peered out of holes – and

Bane never said anything about them, so Snibril thought it better not to ask. Some things were best left untalked about.

Suddenly – 'Look!' yelled Pismire. The carts had rounded a hair and almost crashed into an army coming the other way.

'I'm looking,' said Bane grimly, watching the army coming up behind them. 'Shiandi and the South-West Chairleg! Both at once.'

'I dread what I am about to hear,' said Pismire, 'but is it us and one of them against the other, all against all, or both of them onto us?'

'I don't think we're going to stay here,' muttered Snibril, as the two armies came closer. Then he turned the cart and disappeared into the hairs.

As the last cart went off the path the two armies came round the corner.

'You!' said the Shiandian commander.

'You!' said the South-West Chairleg commander.

All thoughts of the people were forgotten as the two armies rushed forward to do battle.

Meanwhile, getting further away every second, the carts rumbled down a long slope so fast that the bounders hardly touched the ground.

'Where are we going?' yelled Pismire above the rushing wind.

'I only wish I knew,' said Snibril.

Ahead of them a hole appeared in the Carpet, and the carts entered a large gloomy cavern. Here and there tiny lights appeared, as people lit torches, and soon a string of lights was winding through the caves.

'Where is this?' whispered Glurk, and his voice echoed from black wall to black wall.

'I recognize it,' said Pismire. 'These are the

caves of Underlay, the land beneath the Carpet. Come and look.'

Snibril and Pismire left the cart, and padded over to a cave wall.

'Look,' Pismire said, holding up a torch.

All over the wall were strange paintings, some of animals Snibril had never seen, but most of creatures like snargs and bounders. There was a crude drawing of a snarg hunt and, among the hairy stalagmites and stalactites, a picture of a Carpet-dweller holding a club.

'There were caves like this near the Fallen Matchstick,' said Pismire, 'but none so grand. No one knows when the pictures were drawn, but it must have been a long time ago. They say our ancestors lived down here, once.'

They travelled for days in the darkness of the

caves, following the main caverns.

Then one day they came to a place where the cave branched into three. 'What now?' said Glurk. 'We're lost as it is.'

'I don't think so. Come and look at this.' Snibril was standing by the left-hand cave, looking at something. Scratched on the rock were the letters:

R (THE W.) II

'Robinson the Wanderer! Pismire's great-great-grandfather was here!'

'Of course. He was the one who first found the Land. But what about "II"?'

'That must mean two inches. Only two inches to go! Why, we could do it in a few days!'

Only two inches to go. It was a good job too.

The cartwheels were cracked and broken, half the provisions had been lost, and the people could hardly walk another step. But the thought of the land to come helped them as they pushed and pulled the creaking carts through the dim, flickering caverns of Underlay, singing the triumphant battle-song of the Fallen Matchstick:

'O'er Weft and Weave,
Warp and Woof,
The Fallen Matchstick people proudly sing,
Because of their well-known prowess
With their famous bows,
Which are bent hair
Fastened with string.'

But they sang it in the old Carpet-language, which sounded a lot better.*

* But not much. Unless you are a tone-deaf snarg.

Bane and Snibril trudged up the slope, where a tiny point of light showed the distant opening.

Neither said a word, but Snibril knew that Bane would be leaving them when the new land was reached. What things Bane had seen, what places he had been to! He had wandered over most of the Carpet, even seen the great and shiny plains of the Linoleum. As the mood took him he had been a soldier, a hair-jack, a hunter, an explorer – he had lit his campfire in places where even fire was unknown. He could not be expected to stay anywhere long, and Snibril felt sad.

Then – 'Look,' said Bane.

They had come to the end of the caves, and were standing on a ledge from which a natural pathway led down. Before them was the Land. Tall hairs grew thickly about them, with cool glades where herds of strange animals grazed, and overhead the light filtered down to make a pattern on the Carpet floor.

'It's beautiful,' said Snibril.

'It's yours,' said Bane.

'Yours too.'

'No. In a way the whole Carpet is mine, but a single part of it cannot be.' And, suddenly, Bane was gone.

That evening the people lit a great celebration bonfire, but Snibril did not celebrate.

He sat in the shadows with Pismire, half dreaming of the unexplored regions of the Carpet. Pismire looked at him, and understood.

'You know,' he said innocently, 'I think the people will settle down very nicely here. Glurk would make a very good headman. And I – look, do I have

to shout it at you? You know you can't stay here now, you've seen too much of the Carpet and caught the wandering fever. Go now, and don't stop to say goodbye. I've left a pack for you on the cart.'

Snibril looked at him for a moment, smiled, and was gone.

Later, when the celebration had really got going, they called on Snibril to make a speech, and could not find him.

But away in the Carpet, a running figure caught up with another who was stomping along with a great gun over his shoulder.

'I was expecting you,' he said.

HERCULES THE TORTOISE

It was the end of March – in fact about quarter to April – when the smell of spring broke into the shed. It drifted across the floor, found its way under a pile of old packing cases, and stopped at a large wooden box. The box smelled of autumn straw and deep in the heart of it something began to stir.

Or rather, some*one*.

Hercules awoke from dreams of lettuce fields under a midsummer sun. Slowly his wrinkled head poked out of his shell. He sniffed, and **yawned**, and tried to **wriggle** deeper into the straw. But it was no use.

Spring again, he thought. Without a doubt. And he tried to get his head round so that he could see his shell, because tortoises have rings on their shells and grow one for every year. Yes, there it was, the new ring, and Hercules felt ready to face the outside world.

He didn't have long to wait before the lid of the box was opened. A large pair of hands lifted him out and put him in the garden.

Hercules's garden was wide and consisted mostly of lawns, on which a few tasty dandelion leaves were always to be found. There were roses

and lupins in the flower bed – a good feed if he were ever allowed to get at them – and at the far end of the garden was the winter shed and the compost heap. What lay beyond it he did not know. On sunny days, when the wind was in the south, he would explore that way, but someone always found him and brought him back.*

Hercules lay on the lawn and stretched his legs. The hands put a small heap of lettuce leaves in front of him, and he chewed them thoughtfully. The land beyond the shed had occupied his dreams during the long winter sleep.

I Wonder What Lies Beyond, he mused, thinking – as he often did – in capital letters. There Might be Lettuce. Or Even Buttercups. But secretly he knew that it was not buttercups he was after – he really wanted to travel beyond the shed to see what lay on the other side. He didn't think of

* You have probably all heard of the race between a tortoise and a hare that was won by the tortoise. Well, it certainly wasn't Hercules in that race.

it as escaping from the garden.

But the people did, when they found him gone from the lawn.

They looked high and low in all his usual sleeping places, in his wooden house in the rockery, and Hercules was nowhere to be seen.

In fact, he was behind the shed, scratching away at the earth with his powerful forefeet, until he was able to scrape under the wire netting fence. The wind was in the south, and Hercules felt the wanderlust of all tortoises in his blood! He *swished* through the long grass and soon the garden was empty.

'Well, that's Done It,' said Hercules to himself, as he plodded on through the long grass beyond the garden. **'I'm Out in the World.'**

'All right, all right,' said someone, 'don't walk all over me, you great tank! What sort of a

snail are you, anyway?'

Hercules looked down. There, sitting on a dock leaf, was a large yellow snail.

'I'm Extremely Sorry,' he mumbled. 'I'm a Tortoise. I do Apologize.'

'Oh. Hm. I'm Pod,' said the snail. 'Hm, that's a nice house you've got on your back there.* Very nice. I like it. Yes, I really think I do. I haven't seen you before.'

'I'm from the Garden,' said Hercules, 'but I've come to Explore.'

'Oh? Hm, well, I don't get around much. I've only got one leg, you see,' said Pod. 'Just the one. I really have. And a house to carry. It's rather sad.'

'Oh. Dear. If you Climb on my Back I'll give You a Lift,' said Hercules. And Pod slid off the leaf and took up position on the top of his shell.

'Why do you use so many capital letters?'

* To Pod the snail, Hercules's shell would have been like moving into a palace after living in a small hut.

he asked, as they moved on.

'All Tortoises Do,' said Hercules. 'Traditional. You know.'

As he swished through the grass, Pod told him about the world. There was the garden, and the field, and somewhere in the field was a pond. And that was the end of it.

'There's no more. Leastways, not that I've heard,' he said. 'And there are frogs in the pond and snakes in the grass,' he went on, adding with a shiver, 'particularly **one nasty adder.**' He brightened up. 'But also bees in the pollen and sometimes pigs in the clover.'

Clover made Hercules feel hungry, and they stopped by a large clump of it for a meal. It was nearly midday.

'If you want to know a bit more about the world you ought to go and see Old Mother Greengroan,'

said Pod, with his mouth full. 'She lives by the pond in the middle of the field. She's very old. Knows everything. Everything worth knowing, anyway.'

'How far away is the Pond?' asked Hercules.

Pod looked blank. 'Oh, some way away,' he said. 'Distances don't mean much to me, I'm afraid.'

Bees whizzed by like tiny aeroplanes as Hercules trundled on, in search of the pond and Old Mother Greengroan.

But a little way behind them a long sleek shape slid through the grass with hardly a sound. Its back was zigzagged with yellow and black, and its little cruel eyes were fastened hungrily on the retreating tortoise. It was the **adder!**

Hercules and Pod reached the pond just as the sun was setting. They stood on the bank and peered down into the deep water. A passing moorhen saw them and hastily paddled off.

'I have some relatives here,' said Pod conversationally. 'Water snails, you know.'

'Does Old Mother Greengroan live Here?' asked Hercules.

'Round the other side,' said Pod. 'You'll always find Old Mother Greengroan there. She never goes far these days.'

'Um. What Sort of a Thing is Old Mother Greengroan? I don't Wish to be Rude, but I Need to Recognize Her,' said Hercules, as he made his way round the pond with Pod sitting on his back.

Pod looked shocked. 'You'll see.'

They came to a pile of stones and dead leaves, where a few stunted thorn bushes grew by the pond.

Just then there was a hiss behind them. Pod turned and saw the adder waiting to strike! It had followed them right across the field!

'HELP!'

shouted Pod, and disappeared into his shell.

'Eh?' said Hercules, and then he saw the snake. There was a hiss and he too disappeared into his shell with a **snap**.

'It's going to eat Old Mother Greengroan!' moaned Pod, poking his eyes under his shell. 'That horrid snake hates her!'

And the long black and yellow body started to slither towards the pile of stones. With courage he never knew he had, Hercules poked his head out of his shell and bit the adder.

He held on, and when a tortoise bites it never lets go. Frantically the snake reared up and lashed out with its tail, but Hercules only gripped it tighter as Pod clung to his back and trembled.

At last the snake lay still, and Hercules unfastened his aching jaws. Then he realized he was being watched. Small animal heads were peering from behind every stone and bush, and many eyes twinkled in the dusk.

A larger shadow detached itself from the rocks. It was Old Mother Greengroan the toad.

'What is this?' she asked, staring at Hercules.

'He's – he's a tortoise, madam,' said Pod.

'A very brave one,' said the toad. 'But why is he here?'

'I Wanted to See What the World was Like,' said Hercules.

'It's no place for tortoises,' said Old Mother Greengroan, 'but you killed the adder, so you can stay if you wish. It's a big place, bigger than a garden, and a lot happens, and there might be other **adders**.'

Hercules looked down at the dead adder. 'I'd Like to Stay,' he said quietly, 'if There's a Place. But First I Want to **Explore the World**.'

And that was how the tortoise left the garden and became an explorer. There was a whole field to discover! With Pod on his back, he travelled from edge to edge – he even went right round the pond! It was a glorious adventure There and Back Again, and when his travels were over, he settled down to live in the field, digging himself a hole to sleep in during the winter, and going again on his travels in the summer.

But he never had to fight another adder. For all the adders knew of Hercules, the Slayer of Adders. And they slithered away when they saw him coming.

Which was good news for Pod too.

DOK THE CAVEMAN

'What's he doing now?' asked Uggi, the witch-doctor, trying to peer through the crack. The rest of the tribe clustered around the cave mouth while Hal, the chieftain, tried to see through the gap in the wooden door. From inside came the sound of sawing.

'It's too dark to see,' said Hal. 'Looks like

he's got a tree in there . . .'

Suddenly the door burst down, and the people scattered for safety. A great round thing came rumbling out of the cave, spinning rapidly as it rolled down the hill. After it came a small man in a tigerskin much too big for him, and as he shot past they heard him shriek: **'It'll revolutionize transport!'** Then he fell into the river.

Hal picked himself up out of a thorn bush. He quite liked old Dok, but felt that he went a bit too far at times. Being inventive was all very well, but not when it stuck thorns into you.

Meanwhile, Dok was blowing bubbles and trying desperately to invent swimming. **'Arms – out! Breathe – in!'** he cried.

And sank like a stone.

Uggi fished him out by climbing along a branch and grabbing him none too kindly by the hair.

Dripping wet, Dok was brought to Hal, who was trying to look dignified while his wife fussed around trying to pull thorns out of him.*

'What was that?' said Hal coldly.

Dok sneezed. 'I had thought of calling it a *wheel*. It'll revolutionize transport—'

'You said that about that other thing, the *boat*. It sank. With me in it. A particularly deep bit of river, as I recall.'

'Ah, yes, but that was because of a lack of aquatic stability . . .'

Dok shuffled off to his cave, sneezing and leaving a trail of puddles. Poor old Dok! Nothing ever quite went right, ever since he had invented language when he accidentally dropped a very heavy stone on his foot. And then there was the time when he'd

---

* In his view, there ought to be a law that chieftains never got thorns in their bottoms.

stuck a seed into a hole in the ground, patted the earth around it, and invented farming. A wild horse had come along and eaten the first plant.

He sat in his damp cold cave and shivered. Idly he picked up two dry sticks that had come from the tree and, for want of anything better to do, began to rub them together . . .

Meanwhile, Hal and the rest of the tribe went mammoth hunting. Things were becoming harder. On the horizon, glimmering, was a long white line of cliffs. The ice was coming back and it was getting colder. And all sorts of wild creatures were roaming the plains and peering into the caves at night.

When they came back, Hal sent one of his sons to fish the wheel out of the river. As they climbed the hill, Hal sniffed. 'Smells like—' He stopped. Dok would have to invent some more language, especially a word for what trees smelled like after they had been struck by lightning. 'Smells sort of – um – *hot*, wouldn't you say, Uggi?'

A thin column of smoke was rising from the cave mouth. Dok came running by with a dry branch in his arms. His face was black and his eyebrows were singed.

'It'll revolutionize central heating!' he cried.

'Oh dear,' said Hal. 'Oh dear, oh dear, oh dear. What now, I wonder?'

'Come and see!' cried Dok.

The tribe filed into the cave. There in the middle of the floor was what looked like a very small volcano. Orange flames leaped up from it hungrily.

'Well, what is it this time?' said Hal.

'It's called fire. It's quite simple to make. All you need is two dry pieces of wood, and then – there you are! Heat, light and something nice to look at, all in one go. Safe as houses.'

'You invented me a house. It had a roof. It fell in. A particularly heavy piece of wood it was, as I recall.'

But Hal let Dok bring the fire into the main cave, and they sat around it while they tucked into cold, raw mammoth.

'Are you quite sure it's safe? Won't it escape?' said Hal.

'Actually, it's hard enough to keep going,' said Dok, putting another piece of wood on it. As he did so he dropped a piece of mammoth into the ashes. Slowly, it began to go brown. 'I tried it out on the old sabre-tooth tiger up in the mountains while you were gone. Animals are scared of it, so if we put it in the mouth of the cave they'll stay away. I say, what's happened here?' He picked up the piece of meat. It smelled good. 'Hal,' he said slowly, 'would you like to help the cause of scientific progress? Here, try this.'

Feeling a bit of a fool, Hal did. 'Umph,' he said. 'Tasty.' He looked around – there was bound to be some sort of catch in it somewhere.

They dragged the rest of the mammoth into the cave. That evening they had fried mammoth, baked mammoth, mammoth chops, roast mammoth, mammoth steaks and grilled mammoth. Then, when there was nothing left but the bones, they sat around feeling as though they would burst.

All except Dok. He sat there with his chin on his hands, frowning. They could see that he was inventing a new word.

'**Coo—**' he said.

'Koo?' suggested Hal. 'Collar? Camp?'

'**Nonononono. No. Coo-coo-cookery!**'

So *cookery* it became. They were so busy talking about it that they didn't notice a spark float up and land on the heap of leaves that was Uggi's bed. Until Uggi sat down on it. He was an old man, but he could move fast.

'It bit me!'

Whumph! The bed flared up, setting fire to all the others. They ran from the cave but the fire went with them, burning up the grass and trees. Suddenly the whole forest was alight.

Hal and the others stood waist-deep in the river, watching the flames.

'It was a good cave,' he said. 'The ground was nice and soft.'

'Where's Dok?' said Uggi. 'He left the cave, I know.'

'Gone for good, I hope,' said Hal.

And poor old Dok, hiding in the reeds, heard him. Sadly he loaded up his canoe with the wheel, dry fire-sticks and one or two inventions he was working on. Then, his paddles making little rings in the dark water, he floated off down the great river. Soon the fire was nothing more than a red glow on the horizon.

After the fire had burned up most of the hunting lands around their home, Hal's tribe had to move on. Far away in the north the great ice glaciers were moving and it was beginning to snow.

They plodded on down the Great River, dragging their few possessions behind them on crude sleds, because none of them could remember exactly what the wheel looked like. And when darkness fell they had to climb trees and shiver, because only Dok knew the secret of fire. And Dok was gone.

They called out to him once or twice, but all that came back were echoes.

'He must have gone down to the sea itself,' said Hal, 'and they say there are all kinds of monsters there.'

And they all thought of poor Dok, all alone. He would have known what to do to catch wild animals in the snow, or to light a fire without wood.

The tribe sat down under a ledge of rock, and

the only sound was the chattering of two dozen pairs of teeth. There was nothing to make a fire with, even if they knew how.

'Uggi?'

'Yes?'

'What's this black rock?' Hal held it out.

'I don't know. It's called coal, I think. There's lots of it around, but it's absolutely useless. Bung it away.'

Hal wrapped his furs around himself and watched the snow, wondering what Dok was doing at this moment.

The next day dawned clear and frosty.

And the wolf pack found them. They were prehistoric wolves, which was bad, and they were hungry, which was worse. Like Hal, they were looking for food. They sat around the rock ledge with their tongues hanging out.

'Uggi, Wug, Dal, Ut and Rodney, come with me,' said Hal wearily. 'The rest of you, stay here.' Picking up his club, he strode out to meet the wolves. The leader of the pack crouched down, ready to leap.

And as it sprang at Hal, a stick whistled through the air and hit the wolf in the neck.

'Having a bit of trouble?' said Dok. In one

hand he held a bent piece of wood, with a string stretched across it; in the other, a small stick with a stone point. **'It'll revolutionize hunting!'** he cried, as he shot another wolf. The rest ran for their lives.

'Where did you come from?' gasped Hal.

'Oh, I've built myself a little place down by the river. Handy for the fishing, you know. With nets. They'll revolutionize the industry. Makes a change from mammoth, and tiger, and all the rest, however you cook them. Like my coat? Wool. There's these things called sheep, and if you chase them for long enough—'

'Stop!' said Hal. 'Have you got a fire there?'

'Several.'

So they decided that Dok had learned his lesson, and allowed him back into the tribe. Soon, a few more houses grew up, and became a village and later a town, down by the big river.

Dok sat alone in his house. He was growing old, but he was working on his greatest invention. Suddenly he sat up.

'His-his-history!'

he cried. 'I declare the Stone Age at an end. History will start from tomorrow!'

And so it has been ever since.

THE BIG RACE

Gas and electricity are tricky things. They leak. If you've ever stood by an electric light socket with the bulb out you can almost feel the electricity leaking out all over the room. It's the same with gas, except it's more likely to go bang.

Now steam is a different matter. You can see steam and it does what it's told; it's like thin water and you can put it in pipes.

Over a hundred years ago steam was all the rage. The Gritshire Steam Typewriter and Laundry Company had a big factory at East Slate and they turned out things driven by steam. There were the famous steam typewriters, steam clocks, steam boot cleaners and even steam toothbrushes. There were lights made by passing steam over red-hot coke – it works – and there was even talk of a steam-driven washing machine. Things were really steamed up.

'Steam,' said Sir Henry Toggitt, sticking his thumbs in his waistcoat, 'is here to stay.'

Sir Henry was the managing director of the company, so you can imagine his annoyance when he read in his paper next day that someone had made a car that ran on petrol. He called the company's inventors together.

'What's this all about?' he said. 'Petrol's no good for anything. You can't make it do anything – can you?'

All the inventors shifted uneasily and started mumbling.

'Well, sir,' said one, 'it's not impossible—'

'Then build a steam car!' said Sir Henry. 'Steam is here to stay! We've put the electric people out of business; now we'll do the same for this petrol-driven thing! Build a car, and we'll challenge it to a race around Gritshire.'

So they got to work. The story appeared in the papers and all sorts of inventors drove into Gritshire in their cars. There were some driven by soda, some by compressed air, and one driven by clockwork.

'You see, Sir Henry,' said Norman Spindrift, his chief engineer. 'It's a challenge. Baron von Teu has brought his petrol-driven car to race ours, but all these other people want to see if they can beat the both of us. And whoever wins, you know, all the big factories will make his kind of car.'

The course ran all round Gritshire several times. The County Council officials measured it out – it was five hundred miles long in total – and preparations went ahead for the big race, while the inventors stayed in East Slate's hotels and worked on their cars. And then the Mayor of Blackbury announced a prize of £10,000 – and a big shiny cup – for the winner!

*

On the morning of the race Sir Henry Toggitt helped Norman Spindrift push their new car to the starting line. It was a magnificent creation of boilers and pipes, all painted white and gold. It had four big steel wheels and, since it was driven by steam, towed a little coal tender behind it.

'If this doesn't win, I'll eat my hat,' said Sir Henry, who was wearing a straw hat just in case. 'What's it called?'

'The *Spirit of Gritshire*,' said Norman.

Next to the steam car stood Baron von Teu's petrol-driven one, specially brought over from Prussia for the race. It was bright red with black Maltese crosses on its bonnet, and the baron and his assistant were already aboard. It was called *Gerta*.

Behind that was the clockwork-driven car, with its eight drivers still hauling on the big key. Then there was an electric car, an elastic-driven car, a compressed-air lorry, a hot air balloon-powered bus and two sail-powered bicycles.

'Resign now – you all might as well,' shouted the baron through a megaphone.

'I don't trust him,' whispered Sir Henry. 'I think

I shall come with you. After all, if we win we'll be able to make steam cars for the whole country.'

Just then the Mayor of Blackbury climbed into the starter's box and the crowd cheered. His speech went on for quite a long time* and I won't bore you with it all, but he ended: 'The course is three times round Gritshire and we've posted men all over the place to make sure you don't cheat, if you'll excuse me. Eyes on the starting flag please.

Ready, steady . . .
w-a-i-t f-o-r i-t, w-a-i-t
f-o-r i-t . . . Go!'

In a cloud of steam and fumes the *Spirit of Gritshire* and the baron's red car roared off. The sail bicycles fell over, the elastic-driven car went

---

* Give somebody a gold medallion and a big floppy hat and suddenly every speech becomes twice as long. It happens to headteachers too, I believe.

twang! and backwards, and the hot air balloon-powered bus floated away.

Hanging on for dear life, its driver saw the white car and the red car zoom neck-and-neck out of the town. They turned at the crossroads and disappeared in the direction of Slate Old Town, their crews yelling insults at each other. Behind them, going at a good lick, was the clockwork car,

its giant spring still unwinding.

Gerta, Baron von Teu's petrol-driven car, roared out of Slate Old Town with the *Spirit of Gritshire* a few metres behind it. The baron was bent low over his steering wheel, and making faces in the driving mirror.

'Hans,' he said to his assistant. 'Get the £10,000 prize money we must.'

'*Ja*,' said Hans.

'I have a plan . . .' And so the baron put his foot down hard and pulled away from the other car.

The plan worked like this. All around Gritshire there were red marker arrows by the road to help the drivers stay on course. It was the work of a moment for Hans to jump out of the car, turn one of the arrows to point down a little side road, leap back in again and be away, before the *Spirit of Gritshire* came hurtling round the corner.

The baron laughed so much he almost felt good-tempered. 'Where – where did the lane go to?' he managed to gasp.

'Slate Chicken Farm!' wheezed Hans, biting his handkerchief to stop himself laughing, while the car roared up the road alone.

Suddenly the hedge seemed to explode and something whizzed out onto the road right in front of the car. All that could be seen under a mass of

wire, hens, feathers, eggs and chicken coops were four wheels and a chimney.

The baron **CRASHED** into a broken coop and an egg landed on his head. He sat there screaming with rage while the *Spirit of Gritshire* disappeared up the road. Worse was to come. There was a purring noise behind them, and out of the hedge came all the other cars in the race.

That night, Sir Henry and his assistant, Norman Spindrift, stayed at the King's Legs in Blackbury, with the steam-powered car parked outside the door.

In the middle of the night *Gerta* pulled up outside the pub. Hans got out and, opening the bonnet of the steam car, did something to the engine. Then he went round all the other cars and there was the sound of important bits being removed.

As dawn began to break, he got back in the car. Their laughter dying away in the distance, he and the baron chugged away.

A little way down the road, a tramp having a quiet sleep under the hedge was woken up by the sound of evil laughter. There was a whizzing noise and a large bag of assorted cogwheels, pipes, springs and other essential machinery flew over the hedge and hit him on the head!

'This is terrible!' said Sir Henry.

It was morning and all the competitors in the Great Gritshire Road Race stood around outside the King's Legs in Blackbury.

I say 'all', but Baron von Teu wasn't there. He'd driven on through the night – after sabotaging all the other cars. They were parked in the hotel courtyard and every one had a bit of machinery missing.

'The rotten rotter,' said Sir Henry. 'Can you repair it?'

'Not without going all the way back to East Slate for my tools,' said Norman.

Just then a figure appeared round the corner. He wore a long grey overcoat and a green hat, with a great grey beard in between the two. But what really caught the eye was the collection of ironmongery that hung all over him – a big drum, cymbals on knees and elbows, a harmonica, bells on the hat, a piece of linoleum under one arm and a tuba around the waist.

'Well, well,' said Sir Henry. 'I haven't seen a

one-man band since I was a nipper.'

But with a cry Norman Spindrift leaped up and rushed down the road, returning with the tramp held by one ear.

'Oi,' said the tramp.

'Look,' said Norman. 'He's banging the drum with a piston out of our engine!'

'That thing he's using as a whistle is our exhaust pipe!' said the driver of the gas bus. And all the other drivers started to shout as they identified bits of their cars.

'Where did you get all these, you wretched wretch?' bellowed Sir Henry.

'Search me, guv. I was having a quiet kip under the hedge last night when someone bunged them on top of me – leggo of my lughole!'

'Leggo his lughole – I mean let go of his ear,' said Sir Henry thoughtfully. 'More of the baron's evil doings, I see. How would you like fifty pounds for your band, my man.'

'Well, it's by way of being my living, guv . . .'

'A hundred pounds.'

'Done!'

It was the work of about half an hour to fit all the pieces back into the cars and drive on. The one-man band, who said his name was Ron Snipe, rode on the *Spirit of Gritshire*'s coal tender and played tunes on the tuba.

*

Several hours later Baron von Teu woke up. He was sleeping in a cornfield miles up the road, because, of course, he didn't expect any of the others to catch him up.

He nudged Hans. 'I thought I heard the cursed steam-car hoot,' he said.

'Impossible.'

Whoop! Whoop!

'Quick, quick, quick! Where's the starting handle! Get off my foot! Gah! Hurry!'

The petrol-driven car *Gerta* roared off in a cloud of dust.

*

The *Spirit of Gritshire* was nearing the end of the race. But she still had to pass through the deep Dankly Gorge in the Gritshire mountains . . . where the baron had another surprise in store.

When the newly repaired cars roared into Dankly Gorge, the *Spirit of Gritshire* was well in the lead, and it looked as though Sir Henry and Norman Spindrift still had a chance to win the £10,000 prize – if they could only catch up the beastly baron.

But Baron von Teu had other ideas. There, right where the gorge was narrowest, a great heap of rocks blocked the road. The baron and Hans were sitting on top playing Snap for ha'pennies.

'Unblock this road at once, you villainous villain!' bellowed Sir Henry.

'There's no way round except over the mountains,' said the baron. 'Why not try that way?'

And with a horrible laugh he and Hans jumped down from the rocks, got in their car on the other side and chugged off.

'The rotten rotters,' fumed Sir Henry. 'I've got a jolly good mind to take the other road and still beat them.'

'It'll take half an hour longer,' moaned Norman. 'There's no way we can do it.'

Then Sir Henry had an idea. 'What about that safety thingummy on the car's boiler – what would happen if we strapped it down?'

'We'd go very fast for a little while and then go off bang,' said Norman. 'The steam couldn't escape, see?' He looked at Sir Henry. 'You don't want to—'

'Why, certainly,' said Sir Henry. 'Kindly tie it shut with your braces! The rest of you,' he said, turning to the other competitors, 'climb aboard and we'll all beat the baron!'

With the safety valve tied down, the *Spirit of Gritshire* soared up the mountain road like a rocket, with all the drivers hanging on for dear life and Norman crouched over the steering wheel. Great clouds of steam formed behind it.

'We're running out of fuel!'

cried Sir Henry, pulling off his scarf and hat and shoving them in the firebox.

Meanwhile, in East Slate, the crowds were waiting for the winning car. Flags were out and the mayor stood waiting with the big silver cup – and big cheque – for the winner.

A speck appeared in the distance. It was *Gerta*, the baron's petrol-driven car, with the baron and Hans waving to the crowds and thinking about all the money.

They were nearly up to the finishing line when there was a growing hissing noise, a rushing cloud of smoke and a blur of wheels and pistons that shot by *Gerta* and disappeared up the road, leaving in its wake a dozen dazed drivers – many in their long woolly underwear, since they had used their clothes for fuel – sitting in the road.

Sir Henry took the cup and promptly donated the £10,000 to the Blackbury Parrots' Home, while the baron turned white and drove quietly away.

A moment later the *Spirit of Gritshire* blew up in a shower of hot rain and cogwheels, and even Sir Henry decided that steam cars were too dangerous.

But they all had a slap-up dinner at the Blackbury Ritz and so he didn't mind too much.

ANOTHER TALE OF THE CARPET PEOPLE

Once upon a time, you remember, the Carpet people made the Great Trek across inches of untamed Carpet to start new lives on the far side. What happened next? Well, the normal sort of thing; they met other peoples, planted and harvested, and settled down fairly peacefully. They really don't come into the long history of the Carpet any more. But some of them went off looking for new adventures, which led to the long cruise of the *Hugo* and the discovery of Rug – anyway, you'll see.

One day Snibril and Bane the Wanderer came to the small town of Warp-on-the-Lino, a port right on the edge of the Carpet. From there the big floor-going ships traded up and down the edge of the Carpet. (A floor-ship looks like a galleon on wheels, and has big sails to catch the draughts that blow across the floor.)

'We've got to find work,' said Snibril. 'Couldn't we get a job here? I've never seen the Linoleum before.'

'Hmm,' said Bane.

A big crowd had gathered on the quay, and a small man standing on a barrel was shouting at it. He wore long red and yellow robes, and a floppy hat.

'I tell you, the Floor is flat!' he

was shouting. 'Any fool can see that! I, Christopher
Pilgarlic, say that if you sail on and on, you're bound
to finish up somewhere else. Now, any volunteers?
I'm afraid I can't afford to pay very much.'

'Catch us sailing out of sight of the Carpet!' said
one of the sailors. 'Everyone knows there are wild
monsters and great dollops of floor polish to catch
poor sailormen!'

'What's all this about?' whispered Snibril.

'It's old Pilgarlic again,' said one of the sailors.
'He's got another of his potty ideas about the Floor
being flat. All I know is I'm not sailing with him.'

When the crowd had gone Bane and Snibril
went up to the captain, who was sitting sadly on
the barrel.

'What you need is adventurers,' said Snibril.
'Sailors are no good on a thing like this. You need

people who are prepared for risky happenings, and you've got two of the best right here. Besides, I've never seen wild monsters.'

'I expect we'll see more than enough of *them*,' sighed Bane. But he also signed on with the captain.

Christopher Pilgarlic was a scientist, and had worked out that, with the Floor being so big and the Carpet so small, there must be something else. He called it Rug.

So Pilgarlic followed Snibril's advice and advertised for

ADVENTURERS, NO EXPERIENCE NECESSARY.

Soon they were surging up the gangplank on Pilgarlic's second-hand ship, the *Hugo*. Some had eye patches, or carried swords and shields, wore furry hats, or had guns stuck in their belts. They looked like the sort of crew who got things done in a hurry.

That night the *Hugo* slipped its moorings and, aided by a slight draught, squeaked out onto the dark Lino. Soon the lights on Warp-on-the-Lino were out of sight.

*

Next day the *Hugo* was alone on the Linoleum, a slight southerly draught bowling it along on its four rubber tyres into the Great Unknown. The Carpet was a long way astern.

Christopher Pilgarlic was at the wheel, humming to himself and watching the western horizon.

Snibril was in the crow's-nest and Bane lay

on the deck. The rest of the crew just sat around and boasted to one another. It was very peaceful, though the *Hugo* was approaching regions where Carpet people had never set foot.

I wonder if there will be people on Rug, thought Snibril to himself. And if there are, will they object to us setting foot there? Pilgarlic says that Rug should be a lot hairier and wilder than the Carpet, so I suppose its inhabitants will be too.

The Floor drifted by, all pretty much boringly the same, except for the occasional small dollop of floor polish with palm-tree hairs growing on it.

Then Snibril saw a smudge on the southern horizon.

'Land ho!' he cried, and soon they were heading towards it.

'Is that Rug?' said Bane. 'Surely we haven't gone far enough.'

Snibril scanned the coastline. Huge coconut hairs loomed up.

'It must be the Coconut Matting,' said Captain Pilgarlic. 'It's on some of the old charts of the Floor. No one has been there for years, though.'

They decided to stop and stretch their legs, and sailed the *Hugo* up close to the hairs. Brightly coloured parrots squawked and flew over the ship, and muffled grunts and roars came from among the hairs.

'A wild sort of place,' said Bane.

Soon most of the crew were sitting on the edge of the mat and eating coconuts, while the captain found their position by taking sightings on the Light Bulb and the Window-ledge.

Whoosh! An arrow whizzed out of the hairs and shot through his hat!

'We're under attack!' he yelled.

'Back to the ship!'

More arrows clattered against the side of the *Hugo* as they climbed aboard. Bane and Snibril peered over the rail. There was nothing to be seen but the shadows between the hairs.

Slowly the *Hugo* pulled away from the shore.

Then round the edge of the Mat came a fleet of war canoes, pedal-driven with wooden wheels. Each one was manned by warriors covered in war paint and feathers, and they were heading straight for the ship.

'Faster!' said Bane. 'They're gaining on us!'

Arrows shot over the *Hugo*'s deck as the floor-ship sped away from Mat. Behind it, the chanting of the warriors in their pedal-driven war canoes began to die away.

Wind began to hum in the *Hugo*'s rigging, and

the normal draught that blew across the Lino increased to a gale. Great balls of dust rolled past the boat. They had been chased into a floor-storm!

'Take in the sails! Take in the sails!' yelled Captain Pilgarlic, but it was too late. Everyone clung to the deck as the *Hugo*'s big square sails filled with wind, and she soared away in the teeth of the gale, her wheels hardly touching the Lino. Monster fluff clouds rumbled by at a terrific speed. Then came an echoing sound that seemed to fill the whole room.

Slam!

When Snibril looked up the *Hugo* seemed to have run into something. Someone was holding onto one of his legs, and Pilgarlic was sitting on him. Half the masts had been blown off. The ship was a wreck.

He looked over the broken rail. They were in a drift of fluff around – what? He peered up. It seemed to be a huge great wooden mountain.

Bane was standing on a mound of dust a little way off, also gazing up.

'I do believe this is one of the Table Legs,' he said. 'I didn't believe they existed.'

'My poor ship!' moaned Pilgarlic.

'Let's get off,' said Snibril.

When they finally got sorted out they found that the *Hugo* wasn't too badly damaged, but it would take several days' work to repair her. When Bane heard this, he began to fidget and mutter. Staying in one place for a long time made him nervous, and it wasn't long before he suggested a small group of them climbed a little way up the Table Leg.

Leaving a party to patch up the ship, Pilgarlic, Bane and Snibril took a few days' supplies and made ready for the climb. A table leg might seem smooth to you, but to them it was as jagged and knobbly as a mountain!

Woodworm holes loomed up as large as caves, and they skirted them nervously. On a narrow ledge, inches above the Floor, they came across a flock of goats with silver bells around their necks. The air was thin and clear, and from higher up there came a far-off chanting.

As they rounded a splinter, they saw, perched precariously on the leg, a little monastery built of dust grains. The monks came out to meet them.

'So you're looking for the Rug?' said the Grand Lama to Pilgarlic. 'I think we can help. We have made a study of the Floor through our telescopes—'

He was interrupted by a loud gonging sound.

'The Abominable Woodworm! The Abominable Woodworm is coming!' someone was shouting.

People ran for the monastery, shooing their flocks before them. A distant chewing noise could be heard.

'What is the Abominable Woodworm?' asked Pilgarlic. The three of them were left quite alone on the ledge.

Snibril drew his sword. 'I don't know,' he said, 'but I think we're about to find out.'

Bane loaded his gun. 'It's the great-grandfather of all woodworms,' he muttered.

'Here it comes!' screamed Pilgarlic.

Crack! Some of the wood fell away as the woodworm ate its way through the Table Leg.

Halfway up, Snibril, Bane and Christopher Pilgarlic hid behind a splinter and stared up at it.

It was covered in white scales, and had a large mouth full of sharp teeth – and sawdust, which it chewed thoughtfully. You must remember that Carpet people are so small that a grain of salt to them is bigger than a house, and the tiny wood-worm looked like a dragon.

It began to crawl over to the splinter, and Snibril stood back. Just as it opened its jaws he drew his sword and slashed at the horny head.

'Take that!'

The woodworm stared at him in amazement, then, infuriated, rushed at him. Snibril leaped aside and, of course, the woodworm lost its footing on the polished wood and skidded right off the ledge.

So Snibril and his friends were carried in

triumph back to the little monastery, and the Grand Lama picked up the conversation where they'd left off.

'Rug, eh? Hmm. Well, it would be very dangerous. There are worse things than the storm which wrecked your boat – that was caused by the Door opening, by the way. Of course, we know that the Floor is flat because we can see it, but if I were you I'd turn back.'

Snibril said that they were determined to go on, and so, to thank them for killing the woodworm, the Grand Lama presented them all with a speck of gold dust and told one of the monks to escort them safely back to the *Hugo*.

Next day the *Hugo* sailed away on its four big wheels, and soon left the Tableland far behind.

They were sailing through a strange world now,

with fantastic sights looming up on either side. The giant cliff face of a cupboard took a whole day to pass. They sailed under a chair that looked like an enormous cave, and all the while Rug did not appear.

One morning Herbert, the first mate, approached Pilgarlic, followed by most of the crew. 'We want you to turn back, my mates and me,' he said. 'The grub is running low, and things are a good deal too risky for our liking.'

'Nonsense,' said Pilgarlic. 'This is a scientific expedition. You've got to take a little risk every now and again. Besides, we've come too far to turn back.'

'If you won't, then we will make you,' said the second mate, Fred, picking up a belaying pin.

Bane raised his blunderbuss. 'I'll shoot the first man who mutinies,' he said. He didn't often speak, and to tell the truth most of the crew were a bit afraid of him. Everyone started arguing at once, and no one noticed a slight bump. The *Hugo* had run into something.

Snibril looked up first. **'Rug ahead!'** he cried.

The crew of the *Hugo* rushed to the rail. The ship had run into Rug while they were arguing, and giant tufts of hair hung over them. Strange Carpet birds with brilliant wings squawked and whistled high over the ship, and between the hairs small bright eyes watched the *Hugo* in amazement.

Of course, everyone stopped quarrelling. The gangplank was lowered, and scouts went ashore to make sure it was safe to moor there – Christopher Pilgarlic hadn't forgotten about the warriors of the Coconut Mat. They were armed to the teeth too.*

'I claim this Rug in the name of – of,' said Pilgarlic, as he stepped ashore. 'Well, in the name

* Literally, in one case, since the man had filed his teeth into nasty points.

of everybody. Everybody's place and nobody's place. Ours too. Oh well, not to worry, I'll tie my handkerchief to a stick. Would somebody like to take my picture?'

One of the crew took a photograph with a home-made camera. It came out upside-down, brown, and a bit fuzzy, but Pilgarlic didn't mind.

Bane took some of the crew out hunting, and that night they had roast deer and fried ship's-biscuits, with egg sauce. Even Herbert and Fred, who had nearly led the mutiny, agreed that Rug was worth discovering.

'I think we should explore further,' said Bane, when he and Snibril went out on deck after dinner. 'There's something about this place that makes me nervous. It's too quiet, only it's the sort of quietness people make when they don't want you to hear them.'

So next day the two of them led a party of volunteers into the Rug. Pilgarlic came too, with Orkney the cook, Henry the coxswain and Dr Plumbley, the ship's doctor. Bane said six was enough for any expedition. They carried provisions for two weeks.

The jungle seemed to close in around them as they walked in single file along animal tracks. Rug was not like the Carpet. The hairs grew together in tufts, and between them colourful and poisonous undergrowth rose everywhere. There was no sound but the squawking of birds and six pairs of feet going *thud-thud-thud* through the hairs.

'You know, I think people would like to come and live here,' said Snibril after a while. 'It looks much richer than the old Carpet.'

'Humph,' grunted Bane. 'And what if there are people here already?'

Snibril was just about to answer when something hit him on the head, and everything went black.

Someone shouted, and the next thing he knew he was lying under a bush with a big lump on his head.

He was alone! Something had happened to the others – there was no sign of them! He looked around. Here and there a small hair had been bent, or a grain of dust had been moved. That was not much, but at least it was some sort of trail. He must have been left in the confusion.

Gripping his sword, and feeling more than a little frightened, Snibril set off at a run. Night was falling in Rug and he was alone, inches from anywhere.

He spent his first night shivering, halfway up

a hair. When morning came he slid down to the ground and wondered what to do. He couldn't go back to the ship, because the only trail he could find in the Rug was the one made by the mysterious attackers. The only thing to do was follow it.

He had a breakfast of eggs and fruit and set off. The Rug was waking up around him; brightly coloured lizards ran across his path, and parrots squawked away high above.

He passed a creature like a sloth, hanging upside down from a hair, and a small family of wombats which watched him pass by in astonishment.

The trail led deeper and deeper into the Rug, and Snibril had to spend another night up a hair. Invisible creatures shuffled around in the darkness and he had to keep his mouth tightly shut to stop his teeth from chattering.

When he awoke a small green parrot was sitting

on his head. It bent down and squinted at him, and then said: 'If I ever get back to the ship, oh shut up I wish I'd never signed on whatever happened to Snibril. *Squawk!*'

'Well, they're still alive, at least,' said Snibril. 'I suppose you heard them talking. Where are they?'

The parrot just put its head on one side, and then flew away. Snibril jumped down and ran after it as it left the track and headed back towards the edge of the Rug, which wasn't very far away.

He was now much further south than the place where the *Hugo* had run ashore. He crossed the track again, and then almost ran into them. Bane, Christopher Pilgarlic and the rest of the party were being marched along by a band of Rug warriors.

They were twice as big as the Carpet people.

Each one carried a long shield and a wicked-looking spear, and as they marched they chanted a war-song.

Snibril followed them, darting from hair to hair. The green parrot landed on his shoulder and went to sleep.

They entered a large gateway, and a town of hair huts came into view. In the centre of it was a golden temple, shaped like a pyramid.

Bane and the others were marched up to it, and a big crowd of Rug people surrounded them. Snibril crept behind a hut, and peered out, watching and listening as a tall warrior in a magnificent headdress started talking. He sounded quite friendly.

An old man then hobbled out of one of the huts and began to speak in Carpetish. 'You – come – from Big Fellow canoe?' he asked.

'Yes,' said Bane. 'Why were we brought here?

One of our party has got lost . . .'

'We welcome you to Rugland. Me, Tumi, went to Carpet once in a floor-canoe. Sorry to bring you, but for your own good. Many more tribes in Rug. We the Rumbelo tribe. Some tribes not so friendly to strangers. Make big stew.'

Snibril was just about to show himself when an arrow thudded into the side of the hut. Tall warriors in black feathers were climbing the walls of the hut town, and the Rumbelos dashed for their spears. But there were too many of the enemy, and soon the entire tribe was captured, including Bane and the other members of his party.

Oh dear, thought Snibril. Here we go again.

He followed the new tribe out of the town, keeping to the shadows.

Snibril shadowed the tribes through the Rug,

dodging from hair to hair, and feeling a bit left out of things.

The enemy tribe took the Rumbelo people and the explorers to their village, where they tied them to stakes. Fires were lit, and people started peeling vegetables – it looked dangerous!*

Snibril hid behind a hut, trying frantically to think of a rescue plan.

'If we get out of this, I'll never explore again,' he heard Pilgarlic say to Bane, who was attempting to loosen his ropes.

'I want to know what's happened to Snibril,' said Bane.

Snibril was, in fact, not far away. He broke into the hut he had been hiding behind and found it was full of feathered headdresses and costumes. He had just had time to put one on when a lot of warriors came in and dressed up for their war dance

---

* To the victims, anyway. To everybody else, it looked like a good dinner in a few hours' time.

– luckily, they all thought he was one of them.

He crept out with them and was soon dancing around the prisoners, making up the steps as he went along. But since he was so much smaller than the other dancers they soon began to wonder who he was. Round and round they went, and Bane began to look very nervous.

Then suddenly the smallest warrior danced across and cut the ropes! **'It's me!'** he said. **'Let's get out of here!'**

What a fight that was! Before anyone knew what was happening the prisoners had broken free and small battles were going on everywhere.

The enemy tribe were so surprised that they were soon beaten and taken prisoner and, a little while later, the chief of the Rumbelo tribe, and Tumi the aged interpreter, thanked Snibril very much.

'Any time you're passing just drop in,' they said, as the party left the village.

'I hope I'm never near this wretched place again,' moaned Christopher Pilgarlic. 'That tribe nearly made stew out of us!'

They agreed to make their way back to the *Hugo*, and were soon tramping through the thick hairs.

It was Bane who saw the old-fashioned threepenny bit first, when he climbed a hair to find their position. 'There's a gigantic gold mountain up ahead,' he said. 'Let's go and have a look.'

Soon they reached a great wall of golden metal, and when they climbed it they found themselves on a coin the size of a field (to them). It had strange big writing on it.

'This is amazing!' cried Pilgarlic. 'I wonder who could have built it? What excellent workmanship!

I wonder whose it is?'

'They drop down from Upper Space,' said Bane, lowering his voice. 'There was a silver one that fell on the other side of the Carpet once. Next morning it was gone.'

They all looked up. Whatever was there was so far away that all they could see was mist.

'Do you – do you think this one will go while we're on it?' asked Snibril nervously.

'I hope not. All sorts of things come down from Upper Space. Gigantic crumbs, for instance, never get picked up. There's good eating in a giant crumb too!'

'We could make a fortune if only we could take some of this home,' said Pilgarlic wishfully.

'Don't!' said Bane. 'Best we leave it. Once you tangle with Upper Space things can get dangerous.'

So they went on towards the edge of Rug, until

they could see the masts of the *Hugo*. The crew were just preparing to weigh anchor, because they thought the explorers must have been killed. They all went aboard and had a good meal before leaving.

Soon the Rug was nothing but a dark line on the Linoleum, and everyone was thinking of home and the Carpet.

'I suppose people will come again one day,' said Snibril, as he watched Rug fall astern. 'It's not a bad place. Some of the locals were quite friendly.'

'Perhaps,' said Bane. 'But there's nothing like going home.'

'I agree,' said Pilgarlic.

'Me too,' said Snibril.

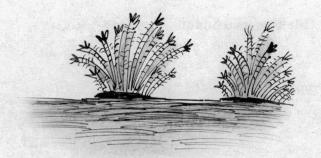

THE GREAT
EGG-DANCING
CHAMPIONSHIP

I don't suppose you've heard about the disgraceful scenes at the Blackbury Egg-dancing Championship? Probably not, because they were really awful. But perhaps I'd better explain.

Blackbury – well, Blackbury is a lovely little market town in Gritshire (Free Car Parking, Early

Closing Wednesdays*) and is built on either side of the River Um. A few miles downriver is Umbridge. The trouble is that for hundreds and hundreds of years there has been great rivalry between the two towns.

No one quite remembers why. But even at the time of the Civil War – when Blackbury was Royalist, so Umbridge of course fought for Parliament – Oliver Cromwell wrote to Charles II:

'Yes, Gritshire folk are devilish bad-humoured and to my mind a bunch of clodpolls.'

Now Egg-dancing is a very old form of dancing and was invented in Gritshire. A lot of eggs are rolled onto the floor and two blindfolded dancers get one look at the pattern and then have to dance without breaking one. It's very skilful and if they've

* In the Dark Ages – oh, as long ago as the 1970s – shops in Britain used to shut half a day a week. And all day Sunday too.

got good memories they never break an egg. This is genuinely true. It's died out in most of the country, but in Gritshire, of course, it's still going strong. In Gritshire, in fact, Egg-dancing is more important than football – and this year Blackbury and Umbridge, both First Division Egg-dancing Teams, fought for the championship.

So, of course, it was like a war.

The trouble was that Jem Stronginthearm, Umbridge's champion Egg-dancer, was courting the Mayor of Blackbury's daughter, a young lady by the name of Alice Band. And her brother Fred was the champion Egg-dancer of Blackbury.

The evening after the Egg-dancing finals were announced Jem and Alice met at a stile in the rolling Gritshire countryside between the two towns.

'I can't stop long,' said Alice. 'Dad's having a big party tonight. He says Fred will soon beat you in the championship and Blackbury'll win the Egg Cup. What can we do?'

Jem scratched his head. 'Well, I don't know about Blackbury winning the cup,' he said. 'But what I say is, I've got a bit of money put by and it's not a bad little blacksmith's business I've built up, with a cottage behind the forge and all. So I'm going to come and ask your dad if he'll let I marry thee, and then we'll see what he'll say to that.'

Next day after work Jem strode along the riverbank to Blackbury and thumped on the front door of Mr Amos Band's house.

'Alice told me as you'd be coming by,' said Amos, when Jem had been shown in.

Now Blackbury people are very sly and cunning and Amos was as cunning as they come. He had been having a good think. Jem stood in front of

him, a bit nervous as you may imagine, twisting his cap in his hands.

'All I'll say is this,' said Amos, with a sly smile. 'I've got no objections to you, you understand. You're a very good blacksmith from all accounts, but I couldn't let my little girl marry someone who'd won the Egg Cup for Umbridge, could I? Not with me being Mayor of Blackbury. I understand you'll be dancing against our Fred next week.'

'What you mean is, if I lose the championship on purpose then you might let Alice and me get wed,' said Jem slowly. 'You mean I've got to let Blackbury win the cup . . .'

'A nod's as good as a wink to a blind horse, I always say,' said Amos. 'Well, there it is, so what's your answer?'

'That's very unfair,' said Jem. 'You know I've

got to try for the Egg-dancing Championship. The whole of Umbridge is depending on me.'

'Well, I'm sorry, but there it is,' said Mr Band smugly. 'Think it over.'

Just as Jem was striding away down the street a badly made paper aeroplane drifted down from one of the upper windows of Band house. It hit him on the head, and written on it was:

Dad has locked
me in my room.
I've had a good cry.
Love, Alice.

It was a Friday morning, and Umbridge street market was in full swing. But Jem Stronginthearm looked so gloomy as he walked back home that everyone turned to stare at him.

He stamped upstairs to the Solly O'Flynn

gymnasium, which was over the bicycle shop next door. It was rather a poky room, painted in brown and cream and covered with fading photographs of former champion Egg-dancers, who all wore long trousers and waxed moustaches.

Solly O'Flynn was Jem's trainer and manager and he always wore a check suit and a bowler hat. He was reading the paper when Jem came in.

'What's up?' he said.

'I'm not going in for the championship tomorrow,' said Jem. 'Betsy Bates'll have to dance instead.' (Betsy was another Egg-dancer: not bad but inclined to break them.)

'You can't do that,' said Solly. 'It's all arranged and everything! I've even signed a contract for you to dance in the Commonwealth Championship!'

But Jem had gone, and very soon a lot of worried people discovered that he'd left the

town – and tomorrow was Egg-dancing Day.

The day of the Egg-dancing Championship dawned and there was still no sign of the Umbridge Champion, Jem Stronginthearm.

The championship was held in a big field just outside Blackbury, and, of course, there were lots of sideshows. The Blackbury Borough Volunteer Silver Band were playing tasteful waltzes at one end of the field, and at the other there was stirring military music from the band of the 1st Gritshire Bombardiers (including their own private march-ing tune, which had terrified the enemy from Agincourt to El Alamein, 'My Old Granddad's Walking Stick'*).

And there were lots of crowds and noise. But there was no sign of Jem.

In the Umbridge tent, Solly O'Flynn was

* And if you'd met the old Granddad in question, you'd know why.

helping Betsy Bates into her Egg-dancing boots. 'I know you won't do as good as Jem, but try not to lose,' he hissed.

And of course, in the Blackbury tent, Mr Band the mayor was congratulating himself on his way of getting Jem out of the contest.

'You get out there and win, Fred,' he told his son. 'Blackbury'll win the cup again!'

Outside, the loudspeakers announced that the contest would soon start. The sound floated away over the roofs of Blackbury to where Alice Band, Fred's sister, was sitting miserably in her bedroom. She had been locked in again.

There was a sound of a ladder bumping against the windowsill – and Jem's face appeared.

'Get some things together, Alice,' he said. 'We can run off to Gretna Green and get married while everyone's at the championship.'

'No fear,' said Alice, folding her arms. 'I'm not going to have people say my husband ran away from Egg-dancing. I'm ashamed of you for giving in to Dad like that. You go back there – it's starting in a few minutes. Then we might see about Gretna Green!'

In the big field outside Blackbury the referee was just about to announce the start of the championship match.

But half a mile away a small cart was rattling over the empty cobbled streets with Jem Stronginthearm at the reins and Alice Band hanging on for dear life. **'I don't know what your dad's going to say!'** shouted Jem.

'Never you mind about that,' said Alice. 'You just get up on that dancing floor and win the Egg Cup!'

As they galloped into the field they heard the

referee over the loudspeakers saying: 'Since Jem Stronginthearm hasn't turned up—'

'Here he is!'

screamed Alice, as the horses surged through the cheering crowd.

Jem climbed up onto the stage and took up his position in the centre of a lot of eggs. Betsy gratefully handed him her blindfold – she knew that Jem was more likely to beat Fred than her.

'Oh – er – well, then, in that case, may the best man win,' said the referee, and she signalled the band to start playing so the dancers could be blindfolded and the dancing could start.

Egg-dancers dance rather like a cat leaping from one hot tin roof to another, and while the two finalists started off with some fairly slow and easy tunes Jem realized that Fred Band was really quite a good dancer. He'd need a lot of beating.

Down in the audience Mr Amos Band was cursing and swearing. 'That Jem is too good,' he muttered. 'If he goes on like this our Fred will never win the cup. We'll have to see what we can do about that!'

After ten strenuous rounds of Egg-dancing, Jem Stronginthearm and Fred Band were neck and neck. Jem had slightly cracked four eggs and smashed one (which meant double penalty points), and Fred had cracked six. Six all.

Up on the stage the President of the Egg-dancing Board of Control addressed the crowd. 'This is the first time in history that there has ever been a draw,' she said, 'and since there is only one Egg Cup we must hold a dance-off to find the winner. After much consideration the committee

have agreed that the tune will be that well-known Irish one, "The Irish Washerwoman". And, er' – she consulted her notes – 'it'll be played at *double speed!'*

A gasp went up from the crowd. That tune had caused many a promising Egg-dancer to smash the lot and tie his knees in knots (it's the one that goes *deedle-dee-deedle-dee-deedle-dee-deedle* – oh well, you know. And at double speed!).

The judge decided to hold the dance-off after lunch, so everybody wandered off towards the canteen tents. Both the dancers looked thoughtful, and Jem hardly touched his third helping of beef dumplings, suet pudding and baked potatoes . . .

Several hundred metres away, two crooks were sitting in an old motor car, watching the field through binoculars. (You know that policemen have 'police' painted in large letters on their cars? Well, the crooks' car had **'CROOKS'** on it in bright red letters – just so's not to confuse people.)

'That Egg-dancing Cup looks as if it is worth a pretty penny, Mugsy,' said one of them.

'Several thousand pounds,' said the other, who was his brother. 'You know, Slugsy, there's bound to be confusion when the dance finishes. That's when we'll nick it. What's for lunch?'

While the crooks were eating a sinister pork pie and a highly suspicious jam turnover, Fred Band – the Blackbury champion – was very worried.

'I'll never be able to do it, Dad,' he wailed to Amos Band. 'The dance is too fast! I'll smash dozens of eggs.'

'Not these you won't!' whispered Amos. He held up a box of china eggs. 'I know it's cheating,' he said, 'but the honour of Blackbury is at stake!'

The crowd was hushed as the two contestants took their positions for the dance-off in the Gritshire Egg-dancing Championship.

A complicated pattern of eggs was laid out on the floor around them, the blindfolds were produced again, and the 1st Gritshire Bombardiers' military band struck up the opening bars of that great dancing tune 'The Irish Washerwoman'.

And off they danced.

All the people in the judges' tent were crowded around the entrance. The gold and silver Egg Cup was all alone on a table. And, held very carefully, a knife was cutting a slit in the back of the tent. Slugsy Nales, wearing a proper crook's outfit (black and white striped jumper, mask over the eyes and a flat hat – you don't see many of them about now), reached in and carefully dropped the cup into a bag marked 'Swag'.

Meanwhile, Jem Stronginthearm was not doing very well. The dance was getting faster, and he knew he had already cracked several eggs. What he couldn't understand was why Fred Band's eggs only rolled away when he trod on them – he could hear them just knocking into each other but not breaking.

'There's no doubt about it,' one of the judges was saying. 'The Blackbury man is pulling ahead.'

Amos Band, Mayor of Blackbury, grinned broadly. Alice Band – who was on Jem's side and was watching from the seat of his horse and cart – chewed her handkerchief nervously.

Since the cart was fairly high it was Alice who first saw Slugsy and Mugsy tiptoeing away behind the crowd to their old car, whilst carrying a large bag with a shape in it not entirely unlike a stolen Egg-dancing Cup. **'Felons!'** she cried. **'Apprehend them!'**

Jem stopped dancing in a crash of eggs. He tore off his blindfold, and with one bound leaped off the platform and landed in his cart, and next moment he and Alice were rumbling across the field after the car.

The music ended in a crash of broken notes. It took a few seconds for everyone else to realize what was going on. Then the chase began!

The crooks' car sped away through Blackbury, which was practically deserted. Close behind came the cart with Jem and Alice Band. Behind them, in this order, came:

- **the 1st Gritshire Bombardiers' Band in a jeep, still playing**
- **several policemen on bicycles**
- **the Blackbury Royal Mayoral Rolls-Royce, driven furiously by Amos Band**
- **twenty assorted other cars and carts**
- **and a crowd of dogs.**

The crooks skidded round a corner and zoomed off down Slade Street. But Jem's cart was close behind and he was standing up and judging the distance between them. Balancing his weight carefully, he took a jump over the horse and landed on the back of the car.

Mugsy Nales turned round with a look of

absolute terror and in a crowded four seconds the car demolished two lampposts, a letter box, a litter bin and a bus stop. The sack containing the cup was thrown high in the air.

Alice Band caught it as it came down.

Jem scrambled out of the wreckage with a crook over each shoulder just as the rest of the chase arrived.

'Well, well, well,' said Amos Band. 'Thank you very much for getting the cup back. It'll look nice on Fred's mantelpiece – under Rule 198, you know, Jem is disqualified for leaving the dance before it ended.'

Before anyone could say anything, Fred Band stepped forward. 'That would be true except that I was dancing on artificial eggs. Dad gave them to me.'

'Fred!' gasped Amos.

'Sorry, Dad,' said Fred shamefacedly. 'I just couldn't do it!'

So everyone went back to the field, where Jem was presented with the Egg Cup – to keep, because he'd won it three times. And when Jem announced that he and Alice were going to get married, there wasn't much Amos could say about it, really, except to arrange with the Bishop for them to use Blackbury Cathedral.

The evening ended with fireworks and dancing while a big orange moon rose over the town.*

* We don't see that kind of moon much these days, but Gritshire has always been behind the times.

EDWO THE BORING KNIGHT

Once upon a time there was a king who had three sons – kings generally do. And the youngest one, instead of being good and kind and brave, was worse than you could hope to meet in a month of Mondays. His two older brothers were quite nice in a rather ordinary way but he was a real terror.

His name was Edwo.

One day the king said to his prime minister, 'I think it's time the lads were sent out to seek their fortune.' This was the custom in the land. (The idea was to find some rich princesses.)

'Jolly good idea,' said the prime minister. 'I suggest you send Edwo to the moon or the bottom of the sea!'

The king scratched his head. 'That's not very nice,' he said. 'What's wrong with him? He's a quiet lad and doesn't mix with catapults and such.'

'He's such a know-all!' exclaimed the prime minister.

And that was the trouble. Throughout the kingdom, which was not very big and mostly consisted of forest and goats, people used to lock their doors when they saw Edwo coming.

If they weren't quick enough he'd soon start off in his boring voice about such interesting facts as the orbit of Neptune or the calorific content of carrots. He was very brainy and might have been quite pleasant, but no one stayed listening long enough to find out.

And so, next day, the king called his sons together and sent them out to seek their fortunes.

Edwo, being the youngest, left last. His two brothers had taken the best horses, so he had to make do with a broken-down old donkey. He travelled east, through the forest, and soon he started to chat to the donkey.

At last the beast stopped, looked round at him and said, 'That's the most boring thing I ever heard. You're the most boring and uninteresting person I ever heard.'

'Well, I like that!' said Edwo. 'You're only a donkey.'

'Ah yes, but I can talk, and that's interesting,' said the donkey. 'All I can say is, any rich princess you meet will fall asleep out of boredom.'

'I can't help it,' said Edwo. 'I've just got a boring voice. I'm not mad keen on rich princesses anyway.'

At that moment the bushes parted and two big green eyes stared at them. 'It's a dragon!' said the donkey.

The dragon slithered out of the bushes and blinked at them, breathing a small cloud of smoke. It looked hungry.

'Hmm,' said Edwo. 'Is it the Great Green Dragon or one of the blue-hued variety? One can tell by the constrictions of the peripatetic tooth-holders that it is about a hundred years of age, but . . .' He went on and on in his boring voice – and the dragon went to sleep.

The donkey prodded it with his nose. 'It's

bored stiff!' he said. 'How amazing!'

They hurried on before it woke up again.

Further west the forest became more open, with lots of little streams and hidden meadows. The donkey, whose name was Pigsqueak, passed the time by singing comic songs, in what wasn't a bad singing voice for a donkey.*

At sunset they came to a crumbling stone tower right on the edge of the forest. There was a brass plaque on the broken door which read:

F. R. GOLIGHTLY, WIZARD

ALL KINDS OF SPELLS,
ENCHANTMENTS, POTIONS.
PATRONIZED BY ROYALTY.
ALSO HAIRCUTS, SHOES CLEANED
VERY CHEAP, TEETH EXTRACTED
WHILE YOU WAIT.

* His favourite, however, began: Old McWotnot had a Farm, Ee-yore, Ee-yore, Eee.

'Oh,' said Edwo, 'that kind of wizard. He doesn't say anything about bed and breakfast.' He raised the heavy iron knocker, and after a while the door was opened by a small bear. It was wearing an apron.

'The wizard's in conference,' it growled.

'Actually, we were wondering if we could stay here tonight,' quavered Edwo.

'That's different,' said the bear. 'I have to be very careful, you know; so many people are after him for money. Come in; my name is Toodle.' He showed them inside and added, 'It's a bit of luck you arriving, because Mr Golightly is in a spot of bother . . .'

Edwo could hear muffled shouts coming from the next room. What sort of horrible trouble could a wizard get into? he wondered. He pushed open the door . . .

At first he saw nothing in the wizard's room except a small bottle standing on a table. Then he saw Mr F. R. Golightly – inside it, and only ten centimetres tall. The wizard was very angry, and squeaked loudly while jumping up and down.

'One of his spells went wrong, and he was trapped,' explained Toodle. 'The bottle is made of Pinhop's Unbreakable Glass, and it doesn't.'

'How strange,' said Edwo.

'Never mind,' said Pigsqueak the donkey. 'Edwo here is very clever. Say a few words, lad.'

So Edwo tried his most boring voice and talked for two minutes about newts. Toodle went to sleep standing up and the bottle cracked* and F. R. Golightly staggered out.

He soon grew back to his normal size and shook Edwo by the hand. 'I'm so happy I'll give you two and a half wishes!' he beamed.

* Hence proving that Unbreakable isn't the same as Unboreable.

'Only two and a half?' said Pigsqueak. 'I look after Edwo's business interests, you know, and it should be three wishes.'

'It's the cost of living,' said the wizard sadly. 'I can't afford more than two and a half. But I'll throw in bed and breakfast tonight, and – well – a three-and-a-half-league boot?'

He explained that a three-and-a-half-league boot was one half of a pair of seven-league boots (he'd lost the other one). You had to hop.

Early next morning they set off again, and the wizard called after them, 'If you're seeking your fortune, head for Globoland.'

'I know where that is,' said Pigsqueak.

'You know a lot for a donkey,' said Edwo admiringly.

'Yes, well, I was turned into a donkey by a witch.'

'What were you before then?'

'Actually, I was a frog,' admitted Pigsqueak. 'Before that I was a toad, and before that I was a tree, and before that I was a handsome prince. I always seem to be falling foul of witches.'

A couple of days later they came, tired and hungry, to the border of Globoland. Edwo and Pigsqueak wandered there all the next day without meeting anyone.

'I'm hungry,' sighed Edwo. 'I wish I had something to eat.'

Of course, the wizard had given him two and a half wishes. A magical egg-and-cress sandwich instantly appeared out of nowhere.

'That,' said Pigsqueak, 'was a waste of a wish.'

'Oh, I don't know,' said Edwo with his mouth full. 'It's not a bad sandwich.'

Just then they passed a large tree with a

233

notice pinned onto it. It read:

Half the kingdom will be given to anyone who can rescue Princess Keja from Wicked Baron Semiquaver, who captured her on his birthday.

(Only bona fide princes need apply.)
Signed, The King

'What's bona fide?' asked Edwo.

'It means genuine,' said Pigsqueak.

'Right-ho, then – but I wish I knew where the princess is now.'

Letters of fire appeared in the air reading:

You could try the tallest tower in the baron's palace, just west of Snowcap Mountain.

Edwo dismounted and pulled on the three-and-a-half-league boot that the wizard had given him.

'You follow me later,' he said to Pigsqueak, and gave a hop. Of course, the magic boot took him soaring away above the trees, and two hops later he was outside the baron's palace.

There was a wide open plain there, and it was crowded. What had happened was that several hundred assorted princes, out seeking their fortunes as they usually had to in those days, had read the notices and come along. They had pitched tents and lit fires. Some of them were doing their washing in a stream. Some were having a sing-song. There was a terrific din. Most of the princes seemed to be about seven foot tall and much handsomer than Edwo.

Up came a prince holding a notebook. He asked Edwo his name and wrote it down importantly.

'You're seventy-sixth on the list,' he explained.

Just then a stretcher party hurried out of the baron's palace, carrying a very dazed prince. A big man with a megaphone appeared on the battlements and shouted, '**Next!**'

'The baron's fought thirty-four people so far this

morning,' said the prince. 'He'll be ready for you about lunch time.'

'Oh dear,' said Edwo, as he watched another prince gallop over the drawbridge on a white charger.

The prince shrugged. 'Even half a kingdom is hard to come by these days,' he explained.

Right up until lunch time, wicked Baron Semiquaver took on – one by one – the princes who had come to rescue the princess. Pretty soon the field outside the castle was littered with princes bandaging one another's wounds and complaining.

After lunch Edwo went hopping into the castle in his three-and-a-half-league boot, holding a battered sword borrowed from one of the other princes.

The drawbridge creaked up behind him. Oo-er, he thought. He was in a very gloomy courtyard.

A door opened and evil Baron Semiquaver

strode out, wearing black armour and eating a chicken leg in a sinister fashion. He held a club in one big hand, but the effect was rather spoiled because he still had his napkin round his neck.

'Fe fi fo fum,' he said. 'Come on then. I haven't got all day. What rotten weedy princes they breed these days!'

Edwo took a hop towards him, and of course the magic boot brought him right up to the baron. He swung the sword at the armour – it just broke, and the baron laughed most objectionably.

Edwo backed away, and turned and ran up some stairs. He scrambled through a maze of dusty rooms, hearing the baron lumbering along behind him. Strange suits of armour stood against the wall, and there were lots of dusty pictures of dignified ancestors. Soon he reached a big barred door, where the princess was looking out between the bars.

'If you're the Princess Keja, I've come to rescue you,' he gasped. 'Excuse me a mo, I've got a bit of a job on just at the minute.' Then he remembered he still had half a wish left. As the baron thundered up waving the club he wondered frantically how to make half a wish. Should he wish for success in battle? A glorious sword? Suddenly the most boring idea in the world came to him. He swallowed hard, and said, 'I wish that the floor was covered in marbles.'

Since it was really only a half-wish, the floor was only half covered. Even so, there were enough marbles for the baron to go skidding and slipping along the corridor until he hit a wall with a bang that shook dust from the ceiling. Beaten by marbles!

Edwo dashed up and took a large bunch of keys from the baron's belt. After a few false tries he found one which opened the princess's cell.

'Hadn't we better do something with him?' she

said, pointing to the baron. He was beginning to wake up.

'What's behind that window?' said Edwo, pointing.

'The moat, I think,' said Princess Keja.

It was rather an effort, but a few minutes later they dropped the baron into the moat (which was mainly mud).

Later that day the king arrived and, after trying unsuccessfully to wriggle out of it, presented Edwo with half his kingdom as he had promised. The baron was sent into exile, and the first thing Edwo did was throw a large party in his palace for all the princes the baron had fought.

In the middle of the party – by which time the princess and most of the princes had fallen asleep after listening to Edwo – Pigsqueak the donkey turned up. He had gone back first, though, to have a word with the wizard Golightly and persuaded him to turn him back into a handsome prince. (Except that he was not, frankly, very handsome – he had looked much better as a donkey, Edwo thought.)

Anyway, Edwo made him a knight and gave him a large estate. Even Golightly himself had been invited, and he was so pleased he gave everyone who was still awake one-fifth of a wish each.

Then Edwo and Keja got married, because that was part of the contract. Princess Keja turned out to be almost as boring as Edwo: she could talk the hind legs off a donkey when she got going.* They didn't live completely happily ever after – there was the time Edwo walked mud all over the palace carpets, and the time the roof leaked – but they were at least as happy as they wanted to be.

And why not, after all?

---

* So lucky for Pigsqueak that he was now a knight as he was rather fond of his legs.

THE 59A BUS GOES
BACK IN TIME

The 59A bus, an old-fashioned bus belonging to the East Slate and Blackbury Traction Company, pulled out of the station and trundled off to the Post Office stop. Driver Erica Grind was at the wheel, whistling cheerfully, because it was early spring and she had just won fifty pounds in the Lottery.

Inside, Conductor* Albert Bream was teaching trainee busman Ravi Singh how to whistle, while Inspector George Norris was standing on the platform by the rear door, watching the scenery go by. Occasionally he ran up and down the stairs at the back to look at the scenery from the *top* deck too.

No passenger had got on by the time the bus crossed the notorious Even Moor.

Now, those of you who know anything about Gritshire must remember that Even Moor is where all the mystery comes from; it is always misty there and strange lights are seen at night. Because of that, Gritshire has never been an ordinary county. Magic things happen, much to the annoyance of the County Council, because you can't put magic on the council tax.

Anyway, the 59A bus bowled along the moor

---

* When this story was written, a British bus had a conductor to take your money and – if you were lucky – help you get off at the right stop. Or the wrong one, if you were rude to him or her.

road, which was foggy even though the sun was shining everywhere else. Then Driver Grind noticed that the road had disappeared. She hadn't driven off it – it had just gone!

Not only that, the whole bus was trembling, and blue sparks were flashing off the handrails. They came to an abrupt halt. She hurried round to the rear of the bus. It's gone all white in the mist, she thought, just like in the detective stories.

'What's happened?' asked Ravi Singh, standing on the platform and leaning out to look.

The fog began to blow away.

'Well, whatever this is it isn't East Slate Post Office,' said Conductor Bream, 'and I'll tell you that for nothing.'

Even Moor had changed. The road was there a few metres away, but it was much larger, and cobbled. The hills seemed bigger and the road ran straight as an arrow over them.

'You've just gone off the road, that's all,' said Inspector Norris, but even he didn't quite believe himself.

'Hey, somebody's coming,' hissed Ravi.

Someone – or some *army* – was indeed marching along the road. The sun glinted off golden helmets and white shields and one soldier was singing a marching song.

The leader of the soldiers had almost marched into the bus before he saw it. **'What's this, by Jupiter!'** he said.

Now Ravi recognized a Roman when he saw one. Somehow they had driven out of the twentieth century and into the first century BC. He stepped forward, trying to remember his Latin.

'All hail – er – mighty Caesar,' he began. The Roman officer was obviously impressed. 'We – er – have been sent by Rome in this new – er – mechanical elephant, to see – er – how the Imperial Legions are getting on here in Britannicus. This is – um – Brutus Breamus, and General Claudia Grind, and Spartacus Norris. I'm Cassius Singhus.' He pushed his turban back a little, hoping the soldiers would believe it was a new Roman fashion.

'*That was quick thinking, lad,*' whispered Erica Grind.

'General Antonius Casca,' said the Roman. 'It's good to meet another Roman amongst all these barbarians. Mechanical elephant, you say. Hmm.'

Soon the 59A – or rather, Mechanical Elephant LIXA – was bowling down the Roman road, filled with centurions all as pleased as puppies with their first bus ride. They couldn't pay in coppers, of course, so Conductor Bream's bag was full of gold coins.

'Next stop, Easticus Slatinium,' he said, tinging the bell. This is a fine to-do, he thought. I wonder how we're going to get out of this.

Driver Erica Grind stopped the bus in the centre of the town, and the soldiers got off. The town had changed a lot. There were chariots and packhorses in the streets, instead of cars, and soon the bus was surrounded by gawping crowds.

A very important-looking man was coming out of one of the buildings and talking to the soldiers.

'I don't like this,' said Driver Grind to herself. Then the bus began to shake again, and just as the soldiers charged at it the 59A disappeared!

This time the journey took longer and the bus seemed to float in a world of mist and coloured lights. Inspector Norris looked at his presentation

gold watch; the hands were whizzing round so fast they could hardly be seen.

Trainee busman Ravi sat on the platform and watched the lights. Where would they land next?

Crash!

Something had run into them, and was cursing in a loud voice.

The bus rolled to a stop in the long grass and Driver Grind looked in her mirror. In the road behind them a knight in black armour was sprawling in the dust, while men-at-arms looked at the bus in astonishment and a very shaken horse galloped away. There was a girl with the men, and when she saw the bus she broke away and leaped onto the platform.

'**Save me from Baron Bonebuster!**' she cried, and threw her arms around Ravi Singh's neck. He grabbed

the bell rope and the bus roared off.

'I am the Lady Kathleen,' said the girl. 'Are you from the king? I thought you'd never come.'

'Er – yes, we're from the king,' said Ravi cautiously. 'Um – which king?'

'Arthur, of course.'

They all looked at each other.

Meanwhile the knights were galloping after the bus, and arrows rattled off the rear destination board – Inspector Norris got one through his hat. He'd always fancied himself as a knight in shining armour, but now he wasn't so sure. Lady Kathleen sat quite unconcerned.

'Merlin sent us,' said Ravi, who thought an explanation was necessary. 'He created this moving castle by magic.'

'Don't make me laugh,' said Lady Kathleen. 'This is a number 59A from East Slate.' Then she told them how she used to be a conductress on a 35 Relief bus and one day when they were crossing Even Moor there had been a funny noise, and the bus had ended up in King Arthur's summer castle at East Slate. That had been a year ago.

'What happened to your bus then?' asked Conductor Bream.

'I don't know. I got off, and suddenly it was gone.'

'What happens when the bus runs out of diesel?'

'It stops wherever it is.'

'Oh dear,' said Ravi. 'We've only got a couple of gallons left!'

Whup! Hiss! An arrow had punctured the back tyre of the bus.

'And the nearest garage is a thousand years away!' moaned Driver Grind.

The black knights galloped up and surrounded

the bus. Soon the crew were tied up to the hand-rails and Baron Bonebuster's men were towing the machine. Lady Kathleen was strapped onto a horse, and the baron led them in triumph back to his castle. He was surprised at the bus, but not frightened, because in those days magic happened all the time.

'Some of Merlin's work, I'll be bound,' he said to himself.

He led them to a black stone castle high on a cliff, and the four bus crew shivered as the heavy portcullis was lowered behind them. They were led into the great hall of the castle.

'Mrs Grind,' whispered Ravi. 'If the bus starts time-travelling again and we're not on it, we'll be stuck here! But it won't go, will it, with a puncture? If we escape, can you change the wheel?'

'Baron Bonebuster is King Arthur's sworn

enemy,' whispered Lady Kathleen. 'If we don't get out of here, we're worse than dead.'

'Enough of that, you five!' roared the baron, sitting on his throne. 'Now, you tell me why Merlin sent you out in this cast-iron dragon thing.'

'It's a bus,' said Ravi. 'It's used for carrying people from place to place.' He watched the baron closely.

'Like soldiers, you mean?'

'Yes, that's it. Just let me go free and I'll show you,' said Ravi.

He was cut loose and led down to the courtyard, where the bus stood. Knights were standing around it, looking puzzled, and Ravi climbed into the driver's seat. He drove it round and round the courtyard, bumping along on the flat tyre while Baron Bonebuster had the time of his life ringing the bell.

Then Ravi slammed all the brakes on, just like Driver Grind used to. **Clang! Dong!** He grinned as all the knights fell over one another. Then he dashed up to the hall, set the others free and they raced back to the bus. The baron's men were all dazed and shaken, and it didn't take long to push them off the platform. Already – despite the flat tyre – the bus was beginning to vibrate.

The mists swirled around it again . . .

When they cleared, the bus was standing on a small grassy hill overlooking a lake. There was a smell of smoke, and on the horizon a line of volcanoes grumbled to themselves. Forests of giant ferns waved in the breeze.

'Well, I don't know about you lot, but I'm going to walk down to the lake,' said Ravi, and he jumped off. The rest followed, except for Erica Grind, who stayed behind to mend the tyre.

The fern forest reminded Inspector Norris of a picture he had seen when he was at school but he couldn't place it. Big shining dragonflies skimmed over the lake.

'I wonder where this is,' he said.

'I wonder *when* this is,' said Ravi.

Oh dear, oh dear, thought Conductor Bream, who was watching a dinosaur heave itself out of the lake.

The dinosaur splashed its way to the shore and peered down at the four time-travellers.

'It looks like one of the herbivorous variety,' said Ravi. 'It only eats water plants.'

'Are you sure of that?' asked Bream nervously.

'No,' said Ravi. 'Shall we run away?'

They backed away into the fern forests again,

 and the dinosaur watched them go with a bored expression.

'So we're that far back,' muttered Ravi. 'Well, I hope we don't meet a Tyrannosaurus Rex – that's *all* teeth. I think that one was a diplodocus, and they're harmless enough. But I once had a picture book about prehistoric monsters and I think most of them are dangerous.'

'Is there anything else we need worry about?' asked Kathleen.

'Bottomless swamps, poisonous insects, volcanoes, hot springs, earthquakes and thunderstorms,' said Ravi. 'Shall I say any more?'

'Definitely not,' said Conductor Bream.

They reached the bus, where Driver Grind was mending the back tyre. 'The hole is rather large,' she said. 'I don't think I can repair it. And since it was a pretty bumpy ride from King Arthur's time,

I don't think the bus will stand another journey.'

'Do you mean we're marooned!' said everyone.

'Yes.'

'Well, we might as well have something to eat,' said Kathleen, looking up at the rack where four lunchboxes were stowed.

So they sat on the platform while Ravi told them all he knew about prehistoric times.

'Are there any people?' asked Erica, after a while.

'Not for millions of years,' said Ravi.

'Oh. Only I was watching that smoke over there. It doesn't look like a volcano.'

They all looked. Several miles away a thin column of smoke was rising above the ferns. Other people? It might be!

'Grab some weapons!' said Ravi. **'And follow me!'**

Armed with spanners and bits of railing from the bus, the five of them ran down the hill and into the forest. It was slow going, since the ground between was choked with the ancestors of weeds and the grandfathers of all stinging nettles.

'They can't be cavemen,' puffed Ravi. 'Perhaps they are more time-travellers!'

'I'll just nip up this fern and have a look,' said Inspector Norris. The rest stood waiting for him while the minutes ticked by.

'**Inspector?**' said Ravi. There was no answer, but something rustled high above them. Something was creeping away.

'Mr Bream,' said Ravi. 'You and the others go on ahead.' He shinned up into the fern before they could protest. It was very quiet in the ferns, but out of the corner of his eye he saw a brown shape shuffling away from branch to branch. Grasping his spanner, he followed it. What had happened to the inspector?

Large blue and green dragonflies zoomed around as Ravi tried to keep the brown shape in view. Then something furry dropped onto his shoulders and hit him on the head.

When Ravi came to he found he was tied up with creepers. Inspector Norris sat next to him, on a wide branch high above the ground.

Opposite them sat a large gorilla-man with Inspector Norris's cap on. It had a knobbly club in one hand.

'Thank goodness you've woken up,' whispered the inspector. 'I thought these brutes were going to eat us! What's happened to the others?'

'They've got away, I hope. Which is what we've got to do.' Ravi looked at the ape man; there

were others too – a whole tribe of them, in the surrounding trees. He tugged at the creepers. They didn't budge.

Then the leaves by his ear parted and an unfamiliar voice hissed, 'Don't look surprised and do as I tell you.' There was a soft *snick!* as the creepers were cut.

'Right,' said the voice, 'now jump.'

Ravi and Inspector Norris threw themselves off the branch and scrambled down the fern. Someone dropped down behind them, and shouted out for them to follow him.

'Crikey, we thought no one would ever turn up,' said the stranger as they ran. 'I'm Arnold Primley, late of the East Slate Sanitation Department. One moment we were going across Even Moor – the next we were in the middle of the Wars of the Roses!'

'We had Roman soldiers and King Arthur's knights,' puffed Ravi. 'I suppose it was your smoke we saw?'

The binman told them that his waste collection lorry had landed in the forest two months before, and then it had run out of petrol.

They came to the lorry, which by now was overgrown, in a forest clearing. Two more council binmen and the rest of the bus crew were there with Kathleen. Ravi had to think fast.

'Take a wheel off the lorry – **quick!**' he said. The ape men were almost upon them when they made a dash for the bus, rolling one of the wheels along with them.

They were struggling through the mud by the lake when the dinosaur shuffled out of the trees. It took no notice of them, but when it saw the ape men it roared angrily.

It was the work of a moment to bolt the new wheel onto the bus, pile in and start the engine. The battle between the dinosaur and the ape men was just getting interesting when the bus disappeared.

Driver Erica Grind drove like mad. The time mist didn't come this time, and instead they were able to watch the land change below them. The forest was whisked away like a puff of wind, a great sheet

of ice came and went three times, hills rose and fell, then the stream that had fed the lake became a river along which houses appeared. And all the time the sun went round and round the sky like a rocket, days and nights flickering like an old film.

Soon the outline of East Slate appeared, and there was only a few hundred years to go.

Actually, Driver Grind (who by now was getting expert at this sort of thing) stopped the bus at a quarter to four in the afternoon they had started off from and drove into East Slate only twenty-five minutes late, which was not bad.

'You're twenty-five minutes late,' said the transport controller, coming out of his office. 'What happened?'

'Well,' said Ravi, and then thought how ridiculous the truth would sound. 'We had a puncture.'

THE ABOMINABLE SNOWMAN

There was once a young man called Captain the Honourable Sir Herbert Stephen Ernest Boring-Tristram-Boring, who was known to his friends as Bill and was very rich indeed. He was also very bored with living in London.

One day a man knocked at his door, pushed past Bill's butler and said, 'Are you Captain the

Honourable Sir, and so on?'

'That's me!' said Bill.

'Well, I'm Alfred Tence, the famous explorer,' said the visitor, brushing a heap of fifty-pound notes off a chair and sitting down.

'Not the man who walked up the Amazon?'

'I am that man,' said Tence modestly.

'Not the man who punted from Brighton to Bombay in the bath?'

'I am that man,' said Tence, swelling with pride.

'The man who sailed across the Pacific on a raft made from mahogany and shoelaces, and discovered the lost islands of Odium?'

'No, I wasn't *that* man, actually,' said Tence, deflating suddenly. 'That was another man. Anyway, look at this.' He whipped out his wallet and showed Bill a blurred photograph of a white blob in a snowstorm. 'Know what that is?' he asked.

'That's an Abominable Snowman! If I had twenty thousand pounds I could go and capture it,' he added, looking sharply at Bill.

Bill signalled to the butler. 'Give this gentleman twenty thousand pounds from the jar in the hall,' he said.

'Excellent!' cried Tence. 'You must come, of course. We start tomorrow, at dawn.'

'Where to? Mount Everest?'

'Nonsense! That's like Disney World these days – the Snowmen are only found on Ben Drumlin. That's a real mountain for you. It's in Chilistan. I must rush, I've got things to do.'

Bill watched him go. 'What a strange man, Twist,' he said to his butler. 'But a genius when it comes to exploring, of course. I wonder where he got that photo?'

'I couldn't say, sir. Shall I pack?'

'Yes, Twist. I think something warm is called for – hot-water bottles, woolly vests and so forth. Chuck a lot of money into a suitcase too.'

They had locked up the house and were waiting on the step when Tence turned up next morning, wearing a blue anorak and a hat with a bobble on it. He was followed by a small Chilistanian man – his guide and interpreter – pulling a suitcase along behind him. There was a label on the suitcase with his name on it, but his name was so long that the label wrapped round and round the suitcase like a long scarf.* There were also a lot of newspaper-men, asking questions all at once and taking photographs while they ran.

Tence waved them aside and shouted at Bill:

'Just get a taxi, my boy!'

Bill stepped into the road and waved his umbrella.

* And just like a long scarf, there was that traily bit at the end that you *always* seemed to tread on.

'Where to, guv?' said the taxi man, as the vehicle pulled up.

'Chilistan, please.'

The taxi man looked puzzled. 'Is that anywhere near Shepherd's Bush?' he asked.

'It's about six thousand miles away. Here's five thousand pounds to start with,' said Bill.

The taxi man paled when he saw all that money. 'Right-ho, then,' he said.

'You can't go by taxi all the way to Chilistan!' cried Tence. 'There's sea in the way!'

Bill leaned forward and tapped the taxi driver on the shoulder. 'I say, old chap,' he said, 'have you got a passport?'

'Yes, guv. I got it when we went to the Costa Lotta for our holidays last year,' said the taxi driver.

Bill told him to fetch it, so they drove round to the taxi driver's house, which was No. 8 Tramway

Place, London NW3. He went inside, and re-appeared not long afterwards followed by a small fat woman in a brown coat and a velvet hat stuck full of hatpins. She carried two suitcases.

'It's me missus, guv!' said the taxi driver sadly. 'She says she's not going to have me gallivanting about abroad without her to keep an eye on me.'

'Sensible woman!' said Bill. 'What is your name, madam?'

'Agnes Glupp,' she said, and curtseyed, because she knew a gentleman when she saw one.

'Twist, just shove the lady's luggage on the roof. Get in, madam. Are you a good cook? Splendid! I can't boil an egg myself.'

'This is all wrong!' cried Tence, almost in tears. 'This isn't the proper way to go exploring! You can't just take someone's wife along! Madam, there are Abominable Snowmen, and man-eating plants, and dangerous mountains and things like that where we're going!'

Mrs Glupp just smiled absent-mindedly.

Mr Glupp drove down to Dover, and before long they were bowling through France.

'Head south,' said Bill. 'Down to the Costa Lotta – it's sunny there.'

They drove for ages through cabbage fields. When they reached the Costa Lotta, it was all blue sea, blue sky and rich people in swimsuits.

'Oo-er, I remember this,' said Mrs Glupp.

Bill bought a small villa for them to stay at and then they all went down to the beach, where Mr and Mrs Glupp paddled with their shoes tied together round their necks – Mr Glupp even took his coat off. Tence, of course, was still wearing his fleecy-lined explorer's clothes, which made people stare.

Twist the butler bought himself a copy of *The Times*, his favourite newspaper, and settled down to read it, while Tence's Chilistanian guide said he wanted to stay with the taxi, where he had made himself a home amongst the suitcases.

'I say, sir,' said Twist suddenly. 'It says here that a party of Arbrovian gentlemen are climbing Ben Drumlin to look for the Abominable Snowman. I thought *we* were.'

Tence almost exploded. **'They'll get there before us! All my work is in ruins!'**

'Let me see that paper!' said Bill. 'Hmm . . . It says here that those Arbrovians have just set out for Chilistan. I reckon we could get there before them. Stop crying, Tence. Twist, find me a telephone.'

A moment later he was back, and ordered everyone to pile into the taxi.

'Drive to Nasti airport, runway three,' he said to Mr Glupp.

Fifteen minutes later they were driving up a ramp and through the giant doors of a cargo plane. The propellers were already spinning.

'How did you arrange this?' gasped Tence.

'I bought it,' said Bill. 'That's the best of being a multi-millionaire – you don't have to hang about.'

'Oo-er, I've never been up in the air before,' said Mrs Glupp. She sat down and put her hat-pinned hat down on the table. Except that it wasn't a table. It was the control panel, and she accidentally moved a switch.

'We appear to be moving, sir,' said Twist the butler. 'And sir, there is a uniformed gentleman running along behind us shouting, **"Oi,"** sir. I venture to suggest that he is the pilot, sir.'

The plane trundled along the runway, getting up speed. The wall at the edge of the airfield was getting very near.

'Has anyone got any suggestions?' said Tence.

Everyone stood around looking embarrassed.

Then Tence's guide, the small Chilistanian, leaned forward and cautiously pushed a lever.

The plane left the ground.

He sat down and bashed some switches.

'How did he learn to fly an aeroplane?' asked Bill.

'Search me,' said Tence. 'When I first met him he was driving camels. He is clearly a man of many talents.'

The plane looped the loop twice, dived under some telephone wires, climbed straight upwards and settled down flying more or less properly in the direction of Chilistan. The radio started to crackle frantic messages from the control tower, but their new pilot ignored them.

Soon they were over the sea, while Mrs Glupp and Twist prepared lunch in the galley.

*

It took several days to get to Chilistan, because they had to land several times to refuel – usually at little desert airstrips, where fuel was brought to the plane on camels. They also got lost for a while around Turkey.

'I've just remembered something,' said Tence, as the Himalayan mountains loomed up. 'Chilistan hasn't got an airport.'

'That's funny,' said Bill. 'We seem to be landing.'

Chilistan is a very small country, mostly tropical jungle, stony desert and mountains. The capital city, Chilblaine, lies on the bank of the red river McPherson, named after the man who claimed to have discovered the country, and it was towards this that the plane was descending.

Fishermen on the bank were amazed to see it drop out of the clouds, skim up the river, bounce onto the bank and come to rest in a thicket of baza-trees.

The doors opened and a small black taxi shot out at great speed. Then the plane exploded.

'Not a bad landing at all, that,' said Tence to his guide. 'I reckon we're ahead of the Arbrovians now.'

Mr Glupp braked as a small man in a blue suit dashed up to the taxi. Tence leaped out and shook hands with him, and there started a long conversation in Chilistanian, which sounded to Bill like a wet finger being dragged across a window.

'It's my old friend Godli, the prime minister,' Tence explained to the others. 'He says he'll give us all the help we need.'

'That's pretty decent, considering we've just set fire to a splendid thicket of baza-trees,' said Bill.

'Yes, but he doesn't like Arbrovians, because he

had an Arbrovian camera that went wrong, as far as I can understand it,' said Tence.

'Where is Ben Drumlin?' asked Mrs Glupp.

Tence pointed.

The mountain rose out of the jungle and carried on, higher and higher until it disappeared into the clouds.

'Good heavens,' she said, 'and is that snow on top?'

'Some do say it's sherbet,' said Tence sarcastically. 'I don't think we'll have to go more than a third of the way up, though,' he added. 'The Abominable Snowmen are supposed to live in caves not too far above the jungle.'

The rest of the day was spent buying warm clothes and hiring porters, and the tropical night had fallen suddenly, like a brick, when they went to bed at Chilblaine's best hotel, La Grande

Magnifique Ritz Splendide Carlton. Twist, the butler, had to sleep in the bath.

Early next morning they piled into the taxi again, with Twist driving a lorry full of porters and provisions. A small crowd gathered to see them off, and a brass band played the Chilistan national anthem, **'God Save Us All'**.

Then they started off through the forests around Ben Drumlin, the taxi nosing along tiny tracks between huge trees full of brightly coloured birds. Monkeys swung through the trees, and shrieked, and millions of insects hummed and clicked.

Up and up the foothills of Ben Drumlin went the little convoy, until the lush forests gave way to pine trees and finally to rocks and stunted bushes.

The road disappeared. There was nothing for it but to walk. Mr Glupp locked the door of his taxi and hid the key in his hat.

'How much further before we find the Abominable Snowmen?' asked Bill, lacing up his climbing boots.

Tence struggled to get his knapsack on. 'Another two or three thousand feet,' he said. 'That's where I saw them. By Jove, doesn't the air smell good up here!'

'Smells like air to me,' said Mr Glupp.

'Onwards!' cried Tence.

They trudged on up the slopes of Ben Drumlin, singing songs. At last they came to a little mountain stream, that ran tinkling over the stones. Bill bent down to fill his water bottle and heard a whirring noise. There was a tiny water wheel in the stream, spinning at great speed.

'And there's something attached to it,' said Tence. It was a small piece of parchment. On it were two lines written in Chilistanian, and Tence translated them:

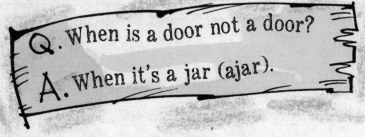

Q. When is a door not a door?

A. When it's a jar (ajar).

'It's a joke,' said Bill. 'A very old one too.'

'Extremely so, sir,' said Twist the butler.

'Hmm,' said Tence, tapping the paper. 'You know what this is, don't you? It's a Joke Wheel. There must be a Joke Monastery up here – and Joke Monks.'

He explained: 'You see, they think the world was created as a joke, so everyone should give thanks by having a good laugh. That's why they tie jokes to water wheels. Every time the wheel goes round a joke goes up to heaven.'

'What singular persons,' said Bill. 'You mean

they spend all their time telling jokes?'

'Yes. They even get up in the middle of the night to invent some more.'

Someone tapped him on the shoulder. It was a small round man in a blue robe, with a bald head and a big grin. Slowly he took a custard pie from one of his voluminous sleeves.

Tence ducked just in time. It hit Twist.

It was a curious scene, halfway up the twenty-seventh largest mountain in the world. The monk stood there, laughing, while everyone else looked embarrassed, and Twist stood with custard dripping into his collar. Then there was a green flash, a popping noise, and the monk was gone.

Twist blew his nose.

'Well!' said Bill. 'What a strange man.'

'That was one of them,' said Tence. 'I forgot to add that they can do magic as well.'

*

For the rest of that day they wandered on up Ben Drumlin. They saw no more of the Joke Monks, as they hurried on past large stones and bushes, although, as the stars were coming out, they saw, high on a spur of rock, a large building.

As they passed it they could hear a sing-song voice telling a joke in Chilistanian, and a burst of laughter as the monks saw the funny side.

'An odd lot,' said Bill, after they'd pitched camp and were sitting around the fire. 'It can't be much fun sitting up here all the time inventing jokes.'

'They enjoy it,' said Tence, lighting his pipe. 'Do you know, they reckon that there are 7,777,777,777,777 jokes in the world, and when they've all been told, the world will come to an end, like switching off a light. There'll be no more need for it, see.'

There was silence while everyone sat around thinking, or just watching the last of the sunset. The moon rose, painting Ben Drumlin's snowy cap bright silver. More stars came out.

'Like a light, you say?' asked Bill, after a while.

'Yes. Or a burst balloon.'

There was another thoughtful pause, and they all listened to the monks' laughter floating down from the monastery.

'I wonder how many there are left?'

'Millions,' said Tence reassuringly.

'Eeeeeeeeeee!'

screamed Mrs Glupp, hurtling out of her tent. 'There's a hairy monster in my sleeping bag.'

'A Snowman!' screamed Tence. 'Don't panic!'

Everyone did, trying to hide behind everyone else as the sleeping bag came bounding out of the tent, hopped high into the air and burst.

The thing inside landed on Twist's head. It sat there, blinking.

'That doesn't look Abominable to me,' said Mrs Glupp. 'It looks rather sweet.'

It was about the size of a football, and the same shape, with a white coat and a small bushy tail. Two button eyes peered out of the fur. Then it started to cry.

Mrs Glupp lifted it down off Twist's head and said something like, 'Izzo fwitened by der nasty man, den? Dere, dere.' Everyone wondered what she was on about, but the small Snowman seemed to understand.

'It must be a baby one,' said Tence.

It coughed and went to sleep. Mrs Glupp

made a bed for it out of Tence's rucksack, much to his annoyance, then, wondering how the baby Snowman had come to be in their camp, the explorers crawled into their tents for the night.

Bill dreamed that a Joke Monk was sitting in a bath of custard and telling the 7,777,777,777,777th joke which would bring about the end of the world.

The monk carried on telling it, regardless of the attempts of Tence to stop him by throwing sleeping bags at him.

BANG!

Bill woke up. Everything had gone dark. Something was treading on his stomach. The world has ended, he thought.

But no. The tent had just collapsed. Bill squirmed about underneath it and raised the flap. A scene of utter confusion met his eyes. Tence was running around waving a gun. Most of the tents had collapsed and everyone was shouting.

It turned out that something large and furry had rushed into the camp and had run off with Twist, the butler. It was also now snowing.

'It must have been a full-grown Snowman,' said Tence. 'Let's get after it! Look at those footprints!'

Bill looked. There in the snow were prints nearly a metre long, each with three toes.

'Oo-er,' he said. 'Oh well, I suppose we'd better go.'

The others relit the fire, and sat round it in a circle with their backs to it, on guard, as Tence and Bill, bundled up in thick clothes and carrying a gun apiece, set out up Ben Drumlin.

The footprints scrambled round rocks, leaped over crevasses, sidled along narrow ledges and disappeared, round about lunch time, into a cave.

Tence bent down and picked up Twist's bowler hat. 'He's in there somewhere,' he said sadly.

'After you, then,' said Bill, who was no fool.

They sidled into the cave. Tence took a torch out of his pack, but all they saw by its light were icicles and damp walls.

They tiptoed on, and there was no sound but their breathing.

Suddenly Tence tapped Bill on the shoulder. At least, that's what Bill thought, until he realized that Tence was in front of him. What he thought then can be represented by a little sum. He thought:

Tence = in front of me.

Therefore he's not behind me.

Therefore it's someone else.

+ This is an Abominable Snowman's cave.

Therefore the person who just tapped me on the shoulder is a—

"Gah!" he screamed, and spun round. It was an Abominable Snowman, a large ball of fur nearly two metres high with the biggest feet Bill had ever seen. And there were other Snowmen behind it.

The leading Snowman stepped forward and said something in a language made up of squeaks and grunts.

'Pardon?' said Bill.

Furry hands gripped them firmly and pushed them along into a cave, lit by candles.

Twist was sitting against one wall, drinking soup out of a bowl.

'Good morning, sir,' he said. 'This is a bit of a liberty, isn't it? They've taken me prisoner.'

Tence and Bill stared around the cave. It was full of Abominable Snowmen.

The leading Snowman stepped forward with a stick in its paw, and started to draw in the dust at Bill's feet. It carefully drew a series of little pictures. The first showed a small Snowman running out of the cave. The second was a rough drawing of the explorers' camp.

Then there was a drawing of Twist and the small Snowman. The Snowman pointed at the picture and started waving his arms about.

'I may be wrong,' said Tence, 'but I think he's

trying to say that they're holding Twist hostage until the baby Snowman is brought back . . .'

'Yes, but we didn't kidnap him,' said Bill. 'He wandered into our camp.'

The Snowman started to draw again. He made it clear that unless Bill went alone to fetch the little Snowman, Tence and Twist would be pushed down a cliff when the sun went down.

'Oh,' said Tence. 'Well, that's clear enough. Hurry back!'

The Snowmen led Bill out of the cave and watched him hurry down the mountain. He skidded over glaciers, leaped over gaping crevasses, slid down great drifts of frozen snow, tumbled into icy caves and, finally, puffing and panting, and with blue and pink stars bursting inside his head, he staggered into the camp.

Mrs Glupp was trying to feed the Snowman on a sort of porridge made out of crushed biscuits.

Gasping for breath, Bill grabbed the little furry creature and rushed back up the slopes of Ben Drumlin. It made frightened squeaking noises, but clung to Bill's knapsack as he climbed sheer cliffs holding on with nothing but two fingernails and a toe. Finally he reached the cave, just as the sun began to set.

'Hold everything!' he panted. 'Here he is!'

There was a great commotion and the baby was hurried away by some Snowwomen. It was the chieftain's son, explained Tence.

The chieftain trotted forward and shook Tence's hand. He pointed at the camera.

'Pictures!' said Tence. 'Of course.'

During the next half-hour he took photographs of Abominable Snowmen standing in formal groups, Abominable Snowmen with their arms around Bill's shoulder, Abominable Snowmen wearing Twist's bowler hat, Abominable Snowmen standing on their heads, Abominable Snowmen jumping up and down and Abominable Snowmen looking serious.*

They didn't actually look very Abominable . . . But Tence seemed happy enough.

'Just wait till I publish these,' he said. 'They'll make me President of the Royal Zoological Society for this!'

---

* In one photo, an Abominable Snowman is making devil's horns behind Tence's head with his big paws. This always seems to happen when photos are taken of groups of people.

Then they all shook hands and set off back to their camp. Twist was thinking relieved thoughts, and Tence was thinking excited thoughts, and Bill was thinking, I wonder how long it will be before the Joke Monks tell the last joke?

They can't have done yet, anyway.

THE BLACKBURY
MONSTER

'Now what we've got to decide,' said the Mayor
of Blackbury importantly, 'is how we are going to
Put Blackbury on the Map.' He took a sip from
the glass of water on his desk and looked around at
the councillors.

It was another meeting of the Borough Council.
Sunlight streamed through the windows of the old

Victorian council hall, and outside the hands of the Town Hall clock pointed to ten minutes to three. They had been stuck in that position for ninety years.

'Come on, now,' said the mayor. 'Do you realize there are people who've never heard of Blackbury? Not of our new heated baths or forward-looking waste-disposal scheme? Our town is so full of history it – er – it – well, it's full of history. But most people don't even know where it is.'

The councillors stopped staring out of the windows and doodling on their blotters. At last Alderman Nigel Lamebucket said: 'Well, now. Tunbridge has got its Wells, Bath has got its Buns, Windsor's got its Castle, Brighton's got its Pier, but what have we got?'

Everyone shook their heads. Even the main roads didn't go near Blackbury. Sometimes a party of vicars would come to see the odd Gothic pews in the cathedral, but apart from that, there was nothing in the town which really attracted tourists.

No one famous had ever lived or died there. Henry VIII once said, 'Where is Blackbury?' and William Shakespeare might have written his plays there if he hadn't taken a wrong turning and gone back to Stratford-upon-Avon instead, but for hundreds of years Blackbury had never really been in the news.

'And it's not right,' said the mayor. 'It's not fair. Any suggestions?'

'How about an arts festival?' said someone.

'It's been done,' said the mayor.

'A carnival of flowers? A big concert? A horse show?'

'Not interesting enough,' said the mayor. 'But

I've got an idea. Supposing we had a monster, like Loch Ness? That would make the people come! And you know,' he said, 'there's every possibility there's a monster in the Sluggard. Well, I mean, we don't know for sure that there's *not*, do we?'

The Sluggard was a rather large pond on the recreation ground in the town centre, full of weeds and mud. People in the park were rather surprised next day to see three mysterious humps bob up out of the middle of the pond for a little while before sinking again.

The mayor summoned a special council meeting, and the councillors stood up and cheered him. 'I got the park keeper to do it with three old tyres,' he confessed. 'Now, let's see whether anyone says anything about it.'

Next day someone found big webbed footprints

near the Sluggard – made, said the mayor, with a pair of his son's underwater flippers.

'Here we are,' said the mayor, opening his copy of the *Gritshire Comet*, 'between the Women's Institutes and a picture of me at the primary school prize-giving. **"Amazing Sights on the Sluggard: Probe Monster, Council Told"**. Hmm, not bad, not bad.' He was sitting in his parlour, with his feet on the mantelpiece, and his mayoral shirtsleeves rolled up.

Mr Patel, the town clerk, sat on the edge of the sofa with his bowler hat on his knees. 'I'm not sure I like this, Mayor,' he said weakly. 'It's dishonest. It's defrauding the public. You know the monster is only three old rubber tyres and a pair of frogman's flippers.'

The mayor looked out of the window. He could see the Sluggard, the weedy pond on the recreation ground. There were at least nine people standing around it.

'Yes, it is dishonest,' he admitted. 'But it's given people something to talk about. And, more important, people are coming to Blackbury.'

And that was true. Ever since the park keeper had first swum round the pond towing the old tyres behind him, people had been arriving in Blackbury. The Temperance Hotel and the town's four pubs were crowded. Mrs Amrit Ghosh, down at the old tea rooms, had invented a dish called 'Blackbury Surprise et la Monster Stew'. The mayor's plan to make Blackbury a tourist centre was working.

Later that day a polite lady from the *Daily Read* called with a photographer, and two professors from Gritshire University went and poked around

315

the edges of the pond with a shrimping net.

Next morning Blackbury was mentioned in three national newspapers, and for the first time in its history the town had a traffic problem.

The council had never really believed that the motor car was anything but a passing fancy, but soon the High Street was jammed solid with cars and coaches. As for the recreation ground, all the flowers and plants had been trampled down by the crowds.

The mayor ordered the local printers to print lots of monster postcards and posters, and then he did what no mayor had done for ninety years – he sent a man up a ladder to mend the Town Hall clock – and for the first time in nearly a century Blackbury stopped living at ten minutes to three.

Bong! Bong! Bong!

Three o'clock, and everyone stopped, shocked.

The clock struck four, and the streets were full of honking cars.

At five o'clock an angry crowd gathered outside the Town Hall demanding to see the mayor.

At six o'clock somebody threw a banger.

At seven o'clock a plane broke the sound barrier right over the town, and the mayor learned that flights from Gritshire airport had been re-routed over Blackbury.

At eight o'clock a crowd of local people demanded that the monster be shot.

And at nine o'clock the park keeper caught a cold.

'Things are getting a bit difficult,' said the mayor. 'I never thought the monster would cause all this!' Someone knocked on his door. He opened it cautiously.

The park keeper poked his head round the door

and then, sure enough, the rest of his body followed it. He was wearing blue and white striped bathing drawers that covered him from neck to knee, frogman's flippers, his official hat, a large amount of duckweed, a white moustache covered in mud, and a clothes line tied around his waist with three inflated inner-tubes fastened at intervals along it.

'I'm surprised you fooled anyone for a moment,' said the mayor sternly. 'You look as much like a monster as my Aunt Mabel, and she didn't look much like a monster.'

'I'm giving in my notice, if it's all right by you, sir,' said the keeper, and sneezed. 'Monstering isn't my cup of tea, sir; it's not what I was born and bred to do. Flowers and lawns, yes, but monstering, no.' And he **squelched off**, sneezing.

Oh dear, oh dear, thought the mayor. He was very good at growing sunflowers too. And all the

roads are blocked by traffic, and the town's all noisy and smoky and full of litter, and it's All My Fault!

For, of course, it was the mayor who had thought of getting the park keeper to pretend to be a monster in the Sluggard. But what now could be done? The damage had been done. Blackbury had become a very popular town.

The mayor put on his coat and hurried out to the recreation ground. It was unrecognizable. Around the Sluggard, the old weedy pond, large tiers of seats had been built. There was also a funfair. All the flowerbeds had been trampled underfoot. A small child rushed past the mayor and left a patch of sticky candyfloss on his coat.

'All my fault,' said the mayor sadly.

Just then a cry went up from the crowd of visitors around the Sluggard.

I thought the park keeper had gone away, thought the mayor.

He pushed his way to the front of the crowd and there, in the middle of the pond, were three loops, looking just like the humps of a monster. He rushed to the edge of the pond. 'Come on out,' he cried. 'It's no good going on with it.'

A large muddy head raised itself out of the water and stared at the mayor through its saucer-shaped eyes. It did have a moustache, like the park keeper, but it was long and green. The monster was covered in pearly scales. It pulled itself out of the water on two large webbed feet and started to hiss like a kettle.

The seats were overturned and everyone ran for their lives! Except the mayor. He stood rooted to the spot, terrified.

The monster yawned, and then two large leathery wings that had lain across its back opened and began to flap in a leisurely way. It flew over the funfair and bit the top off the helter-skelter before turning and flying out to sea.

Blackbury emptied in a few hours.

The mayor rushed off and caught the park keeper and begged him to stay, and then called a special meeting of the council.

'It must have been in our pond for millions of years,' he said, 'but I pity any other councils if it lands in their town. I think Blackbury is best left alone.'

And he sent a man up the clock tower to stop the clock again.

And Blackbury, without the monster, went back to its sleepy way when it was always ten minutes to three in the afternoon.

FATHER CHRISTMAS GOES TO WORK AT THE ZOO

Father Christmas lay fast asleep on the sofa with a newspaper over his face, and occasionally he snored a little. Mrs Christmas was sitting on the other side of the roaring fire, darning his socks and talking.

'. . . And I'm getting fed up! You only work one evening a year these days, and even if you do get paid overtime there's the reindeer to feed. It's

about time you got a new job, my lad.'

'Eh? What?' said Father Christmas, sitting up.

'A new job,' said Mrs Christmas, starting another sock. 'Something that'll bring in a little extra cash and keep you out from under my feet all day. You might even enjoy it.'

'Well, I don't know about that,' said Father Christmas, stroking his beard. 'A man in my position, you know, has certain responsibilities . . .'

Then he thought: She's got a point. I always wanted to be an engine driver when I was a little lad. I wonder what else I *could* do?

So next morning he dusted off his old grey suit (he usually wore a red one with white fur here and there) and Mrs Christmas made sandwiches for him, and then off he went to look for a job.

'Are you really Father Christmas?' said the man at the Job Centre in amazement. 'Well, well!

I remember you bought me a train set when I was nine.'*

'Ah, yes, I recall it well,' said Father Christmas, sitting down. The job man started to fill in a form.

'You say you can fly, but you haven't got a pilot's licence. You go into people's houses by climbing down chimneys, but frankly that sounds a bit burglarous. You give things away. Hmm. Oh dear, I don't know. Very difficult. I suppose you don't have much experience in looking after animals?'

Father Christmas, who had been looking very glum, brightened up. 'Certainly,' he said. 'Reindeers and polar bears and so forth.'

'Ah,' said the job man. 'Then there's just the job for you at the zoo.'

'What's a zoo?'

'They keep animals there, to help to understand them and save animals in danger of dying out. I

* Actually, that year, Father Christmas bought *every* nine-year-old a train set.

imagine it's great fun: just go and say I sent you and they'll probably even give you a uniform!'

Next day Father Christmas went to start work at Blackbury Zoo.

About two hours later the man at the job agency got a phone call which went on for a very long time (just as if the person on the other end was very, very angry).

Just as he put the telephone down Father Christmas shuffled in sheepishly, still wearing his zoo uniform.

'Well,' said the job man severely, 'it's a fine mess you've made of *that*.'

'I know,' said Father Christmas in a small voice.

'You let the monkeys out—'

'I know.'

'You gave everyone free elephant rides.'

'I felt so sorry for them, you see. And the elephants enjoyed it . . .'

'And you taught the hippos to fly. Very dangerous things, flying hippos.'*

'They didn't have any reindeers, you see,' said Father Christmas miserably.

'I don't know, I'm sure. Can't you think of any other job you could do?' said the job man.

'I'd like to be an astronaut or a cowboy,' said Father Christmas.

'Um,' said the job man. 'Not much call for those. How about selling ice cream? There's a job here for an ice-cream man . . .'

Two hours later Father Christmas gingerly drove out of the Blackbury ice-cream factory in a bright yellow and pink van with **'MR BRRRR'** written on the side. He stopped at a likely-looking

* Last seen heading over the English Channel in the direction of Africa. The hippos had got fed up with being studied and saved and fancied saving themselves.

spot and soon lots of children were queuing up for ice cream.

'A small ice-cream cornet, please,' said the first one.

Father Christmas filled it and looked at it in dismay. 'That's not very much ice cream,' he said, so he scooped two more big dollops onto the cone, and added a wafer, two chocolate thingummyjigs and half a dozen cherries. 'There,' he said, beaming. 'You can have this for twenty pence.'

The little boy looked at it in amazement – and soon there was a big crowd around the van. Father Christmas was having the time of his life, building huge great creamy cones covered with all sorts of twirls, swirls, cherries* and wafers. And selling them for next to nothing or even less.

This is just the job for me, he thought happily.

*

* At last! A use for all those glacé cherries.

'Well,' said the job man, 'this is another fine mess you've got me into.'

'**I'm sorry,**' said Father Christmas mournfully.

'According to the manager of the ice-cream company, you got rid of one hundred pounds' worth of ice cream for seven pounds. They're very, very angry,' said the job man sternly, looking at his notes. 'Isn't there anything you can do without making a mess of it?'

Father Christmas, who was really very sorry and quite sad, blew his nose loudly. 'It seemed such a shame to take the kiddies' money,' he explained.

'Look, the only other job we've got that would suit you is one as a gardener,' said the job man more kindly. 'A healthy, outdoor life in Blackbury Parks and Gardens Department. That'd suit you, I expect, and I don't think there's any trouble you could possibly get into.'

*

So next day Father Christmas started work in one of the municipal greenhouses, and for a while it looked as though he was doing very well. Being a sort of old-fashioned wizard, you see, he was very good at getting things to grow, and he quite enjoyed pottering about pruning and planting.

'You're doing very well, Mr Christmas,' said the head gardener a few days later. 'In fact, I think you can plant out the big flower bed down by the Town Hall tomorrow. The ornamental one, you know.'

Father Christmas knew it. Every month or so they used to change the flowers so the colours spelled out names, or made the borough coat of arms, or something interesting like that.

'We'll leave the choice of design up to you,' said the head gardener. 'Something tasteful in primroses, perhaps?'

Father Christmas had a bit of a think, and later he set off with his gardening tools and a big wheelbarrow. He put a canvas screen round the flower bed and set to work. It was getting on for tea time when he stopped.

A few minutes later the head gardener came along to see how he had got on. When she saw the flower bed she stopped and her mouth dropped open in amazement.

'Don't you like it?' said Father Christmas nervously.

'You've spelled out

"Merry Christmas"

in flowers!' blurted out the head gardener. 'But Christmas is eleven months away! We can't have this sort of thing, you know.'

'I thought it might cheer people up,' said Father Christmas. 'I suppose I'm sacked?'

'I'm afraid the mayor will insist on it after he sees that,' said the gardener.

So Father Christmas trooped off to see the job man, who looked up from his files and said, 'What, you again?'

'There was a bit of a disagreement over a flower bed, you see.'

'I don't really see, but anyway, all the jobs that are going now are for steam-roller drivers and bakers, and I dread to think of you doing either of them.'

He gave Father Christmas a form to fill in in case any jobs cropped up, and then the old man went home. Mrs Christmas was washing his red suit ready for December.

'I don't seem to be any good at anything,' said Father Christmas, taking his boots off.

'I just don't know how we're going to manage until next Christmas,' said Mrs Christmas.

Just then there was a knock at the door. It was the job man, very breathless, holding the form that Father Christmas had filled in.

'Why didn't you tell me you were six hundred years old?' he said.

'Is it important then?'

'Of course – you ought to be getting the State Pension! Come to think of it, you ought to get a bit for the five hundred and thirty-five years you missed too. **That'd be thousands and thousands of pounds!'**

'A State Pension?' wondered Father Christmas. **'Fancy that! Come in and have a cup of tea!'**

And so they did.

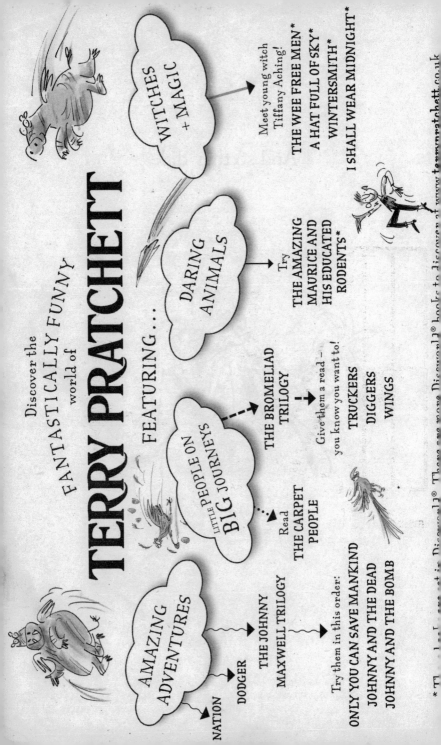

Discover the
FANTASTICALLY FUNNY
world of

TERRY PRATCHETT

FEATURING...

WITCHES + MAGIC

Meet young witch
Tiffany Aching!

THE WEE FREE MEN*
A HAT FULL OF SKY*
WINTERSMITH*
I SHALL WEAR MIDNIGHT*

DARING ANIMALS

Try
**THE AMAZING
MAURICE AND
HIS EDUCATED
RODENTS***

LITTLE PEOPLE ON BIG JOURNEYS

THE BROMELIAD TRILOGY

Give them a read –
you know you want to!

**TRUCKERS
DIGGERS
WINGS**

Read
THE CARPET PEOPLE

AMAZING ADVENTURES

NATION

DODGER

THE JOHNNY MAXWELL TRILOGY

Try them in this order:

**ONLY YOU CAN SAVE MANKIND
JOHNNY AND THE DEAD
JOHNNY AND THE BOMB**

* They're also set in Discworld® There are more Discworld® books to discover at www.terrypratchett.co.uk